YESTERDAY'S FANTASY

Pamela Macaluso

A KISMET™ Romance

METEOR PUBLISHING CORPORATION
Bensalem, Pennsylvania

For my grandmothers . . .

Cleo Lord . . . for encouraging my love of reading and
Esther Barnes . . . for always believing in me.

PAMELA MACALUSO

Ray Bradbury, Louisa May Alcott, and Jiminy Cricket don't seem to have much in common. But this unlikely group—a science fiction writer, a 19th century writer best known for her chidren's classics, and a cartoon character—has been a major source of inspiration for Pamela. "Ms. Alcott sparked my desire to write and Jiminy taught me to believe in dreams. When Mr. Bradbury spoke at my school, I learned that dreams weren't enough. To be a writer you had to combine them with a disciplined schedule of getting the words onto the page." Pamela has set her second **Kismet**™ Romance, *Yesterday's Fantasy*, in her native California.

Other KISMET books by Pamela Macaluso:

PROLOGUE

It was true love, the real thing—Melissa Ellison was sure of it. None of that teenage hero-worship, puppy love, crush stuff for her, even if she was only fourteen. She was in love.

Her friends were plastering their walls with posters of rock, television, and movie stars. Melissa day-dreamed over a picture of Morgan Edwards that she'd cut out of her brother Lucas's high school yearbook.

For two years she'd kept her infatuation a secret. Then one afternoon, while she and several friends were in her room studying for the next day's math exam, one of them knocked her diary off the nightstand. The picture of Morgan fell out.

"Wow." Carol picked up the picture and began to pass it to the other girls. "What a hunk! Who is he?"

Melissa looked at the three pairs of eyes waiting expectantly for her answer. All three of the girls had at one time or another "gone steady," while Melissa never had. With her honey-blond hair and sparkling green eyes she was beautiful. Beautiful when, among her peers, *cute* was *in*.

It was on the tip of her tongue to tell them Morgan was her brother's best friend. When her mouth opened, however, "He's my boyfriend," popped out.

The girls gave off an assortment of oh's and ah's.

"Has he kissed you?" Marcy giggled.

"All the time." Melissa crossed her fingers behind her back. Two big lies in less than five minutes.

Carol, Marcy, and Judy kept questioning her about Morgan. She continued to spin a web of lies. Finally becoming so disgusted with the deception, she snatched the picture back and buried it in the pages of her diary. "Enough. Let's get back to our math."

The next Saturday she and Carol went to see a movie. As they were leaving the theater, Carol grabbed Melissa's arm.

"Hey look, Party Cove has its Valentine's Day cards out. I need to get one for Steve. I'm sure you'll want to get one for Morgan, too."

"Umm, I'd rather wait. I'll help you pick out Steve's, okay?"

The two of them looked through dozens of cards. "This one's pretty." Carol held up a card. It was a seascape photograph with the outline of two lovers gazing out to watch the sun sinking into the sea.

Melissa opened the card. *"Valentine—My Heart Is Yours,"* she read aloud. "Isn't that a bit mushy for Steve?"

"Yeah, you're right." Carol took the card from her and started to put it back. "It would be great for Morgan, though." She stuck the card back in Melissa's hand.

"Carol, I don't think . . ."

"Sure. It's the perfect card for an older man."

Oh, well, she could always save it for the future. Sooner or later she'd have a boyfriend, and it would get Carol off her back for now. "Okay, you talked me into it."

Later that evening they were listening to records in Carol's bedroom and munching on popcorn.

"I've got an idea," Carol announced with her mouth full. "Let's sign our Valentines."

"I'd rather do it later."

"Are you going to write something mushy that you don't want me to see?" Carol's eyes lit up.

"No, I just . . ." Melissa's mind struggled to come up with a plausible excuse.

"Fine." Carol bounced up off the bed. "Then we'll do it now. I'll even give you a stamp."

"I'll just give it to him in person."

"No. It's much more romantic to mail it."

Melissa signed the card with a simple "Love, Melissa."

"Melly, why don't we spray the envelopes with perfume?"

Melissa no longer felt like arguing with Carol. She

silently held her envelope out and let Carol spray it liberally with Charlie. She expected Carol to suggest putting red lipstick kisses on the envelopes, too, and was grateful when she didn't.

Melissa put the card in the envelope, wrote down the address of the apartment Morgan and Lucas shared, and stamped it. She had to tuck it under the top flap of her purse since it was too big to fit all the way in.

The girls played a game of Scrabble, then Carol's mother drove Melissa home.

It wasn't until the next day when she saw a commercial for Valentine flowers that she remembered the card. She flew up the stairs and tore through her purse.

"Oh, no," she whispered. *Calm down and think,* she told herself. She searched her room. It wasn't there, either. If she'd dropped it coming into the house one of her parents would have returned it to her, especially if they saw the name on the front of the envelope and smelled the cologne. She could have dropped it getting in or out of Carol's car, or in the car, or back at Carol's house.

Quickly she ran to the phone, dialed and waited.

"Carol, it's Melissa. Did I leave my Valentine there?" She closed her eyes tightly and held her breath.

"Yes, you did, but don't worry. I mailed it today when I mailed Steve's."

"You what?" Melissa couldn't believe her ears.

"I mailed it for you. That's okay, isn't it?"

"Sure." Her heart dropped to her ankles. "Thanks,

Carol. I'll see you at school tomorrow." Now what was she going to do? She should have been more careful in the first place. She could have put a false address on the envelope, Carol wouldn't have known the difference. She should have thought to tell Carol she already had a Valentine for Morgan at home. Or to be downright honest, she shouldn't have told the first lie that had started this whole mess.

The next few days she lived on pins and needles. What would Morgan think when he got the card? He'd think she'd lost her marbles. He'd always treated her nicely, but he'd never done anything to make her suspect that he saw her as anything other than Lucas's little sister. After all, he was eight years older than she was. Even in her wildest daydreams she couldn't imagine a man of twenty-two being interested in a young girl of fourteen. She always fantasized an older version of herself winning his heart.

A week passed by, and then two. Melissa began to relax. He must have received the card, realized it was a mistake, and decided to ignore it.

Valentine's Day rolled around. After school Melissa lay across her bed, her chin resting on her hands. It had been a difficult day for her, watching couples holding hands and trying to appear enthusiastic when the other girls showed her the Valentines they'd received from their boyfriends.

Someone rang the doorbell. She heard her mother go to the door and then come up the stairs to her room.

"Melly, there's someone here to see you."

Melissa raced out of her room to the top of the stairs, and stopped dead in her tracks. There he was—all six foot three inches of him, one foot on the first step and one elbow casually resting on the banister.

Morgan smiled. "Hi, Melly. How about joining me for a hot fudge sundae?"

Melissa looked back at her mother, who was standing by her bedroom door.

"Sure, honey, but make it a small one so you don't spoil your dinner."

"We won't be gone long, Mrs. Ellison," Morgan reassured her mother.

"Is McCoy's all right?" Morgan asked once they were in his yellow VW.

"Sounds fine." Melissa kept her hands tightly clasped, hoping he wouldn't notice how nervous she was.

Once they were seated in the old-fashioned ice-cream parlor and Morgan had ordered their sundaes, he placed his hands on the table, fingertips together. "Melly, we need to have a little talk."

Melissa was unable to look him straight in the eye. Her heart sank as she saw Carol, Steve, and Marcy sitting at a table across the room watching the two of them intently.

"Ah, some friends of mine are here." Morgan started to turn in the direction she was looking. "No, don't look. Could we postpone this 'little talk' until later?"

"Sure. I understand." He smiled at her, and she felt her heart skip a beat.

How she was able to get through her sundae she never knew. She figured Morgan probably intended to talk to her about the Valentine. She dreaded what he might have to say. If that wasn't bad enough, she also had to put up with Carol, Steve, and Marcy gawking at them. She was never so glad to see the bottom of a sundae glass.

Morgan did most of the talking on the drive home. Melissa sat quietly dreading the inevitable.

Once they were parked in front of her house, he leaned back in his seat, took a deep breath and began, "Melly, about the Valentine . . ."

Melissa looked down in her lap where her hands were twisting and untwisting the shoulder strap of her purse. "It . . . it wasn't supposed to be mailed. It . . . it was an accident."

"An accident?"

"Yes. You see, all my friends have boyfriends." She sighed. "I just got so tired of being left out all the time. So . . ." Melissa looked over at Morgan. He was watching her intently with his deep-blue eyes. The words she'd been planning to say deserted her.

"So," he continued, filling in the blanks, "you created a boyfriend."

She nodded.

"Would I be correct in assuming that I am supposed to be the boyfriend?"

Melissa nodded again as she felt the tears begin to well up in her eyes.

"Listen, I'm really flattered that you think I'm worthy of the honor, but you should—"

"Please," Melissa cut him off, "no lectures about honesty. I know what I did was wrong. I'm suffering for it, believe me." She had never wished so desperately for a hole to open up and swallow her. Losing the vigilant battle with her tears, a sob broke from her throat.

Morgan reached over and tucked a loose strand of hair back behind her ear. "Hey, no tears." He brushed the tear off her cheek, then leaned forward to kiss the place where it had been.

As he moved closer, Melissa turned her mouth toward his. Morgan pulled back abruptly.

"Kiss me . . . please," she pleaded.

Morgan shook his head. "If you ask me that same question in five or six years, you'll have yourself a deal. But by that time you'll be happily going steady with someone your own age and won't even give the time of day to an old fossil like me," he teased.

Tears were rolling freely down her cheeks when she looked up at him again. "You're wrong. I'll never love anyone else the way I love you."

"True, because what you feel for me is puppy love, a schoolgirl crush. What you'll feel for someone else when you're older will be true love."

"How do you know what I'm feeling?"

"I was fourteen once. I remember what it felt like."

"Did you have a crush on anyone?" she asked, a touch of jealousy in her voice.

"Sure—Mrs. Mason, my history teacher. I had this crazy idea that she would leave her husband and run off with me to some deserted island."

Melissa laughed despite her glum mood.

"Sounds funny now, doesn't it? At the time it was very serious. Years from now you'll laugh about this, too."

"Yeah, sure." He was wrong, she knew he was wrong. She also knew she'd never be able to convince him of that. "Well, thanks for the ice cream. See ya." Melissa left abruptly, wanting to reach the safety of her own room and have a good long cry.

Morgan swore as he watched her run away from the car. His "little talk" seemed to have done more harm than good, even though it started with the best intentions.

He had suspected the Valentine had been mailed accidentally. He should have just ignored it, pretending he'd never received it. But if she had sent him the card intentionally, it would have been cruel to ignore it. He'd had to guess, and he'd guessed wrong.

Peer pressure was the pits! Since her friends had seen the two of them together at the ice-cream parlor, maybe they'd lighten up on her a bit. She was such a sweet kid. It had really torn him up to see tears in those gorgeous green eyes of hers.

She was going to be one beautiful lady when she grew up.

ONE

Melissa rubbed the back of her neck, trying to combat the stiff knots of tension. She watched Brian come around the front of the car to open the passenger door. Tall, blond, with an athletic build, he looked as good in the conservative gray suit he now wore as he did in his baseball uniform. In four months he would be her husband. She should be on cloud nine. She wasn't, and that bothered her.

"Ready, honey?" Brian asked, reaching down to help her out. "I'm glad Mother thought of this before the construction crew started building."

Melissa cringed as they walked down the dirt path toward the site where their future home would stand. It was supposed to be their dream house, but it was turning into a nightmare. "I was happy with the choices we'd made with Mr. Stevens, and I still don't like the idea of her paying for the designing fees. I'm sure it's very expensive," Melissa said.

Brian shook his head. "Lissa, I thought we had this all settled last night. Why can't you just accept this as Mother's wedding gift?"

Melissa bit her tongue. Yes, they'd been through it all last night, and she *still* thought linens, china, or paying for the honeymoon were more appropriate gifts than her mother-in-law's choice of hiring an architect to custom-design their home. Of course it wouldn't be half so bad if all the woman intended to do was pick up the tab, but Melissa was sure Mrs. Marshall wouldn't be sitting on the sidelines. Ever since Brian's mother had arrived in San Diego, she had been "helping" with all their plans, offering new suggestions and making changes in the decisions they'd already made.

"Don't forget, this will send our resale value sky high," Brian continued.

"Resale value, Brian? What happened to settling in, putting down roots, and raising a family?"

Brian didn't have a chance to answer her question before they were joined by Mr. Stevens.

"Mr. Marshall, Ms. Ellison." The building contractor shook their hands. "Mr. Edwards should be here any minute. You've made an excellent choice, by the way. The man's a real artist. We worked together on Senator Griffith's house. I talked to him on the phone last night, and he's already got some ideas. Mrs. Marshall brought him out to the lot yesterday evening."

Melissa had had enough. The whole purpose for today's meeting was for *them* to show the architect the lot and discuss *their* ideas with him. As soon as this meeting was over, she was going to put her foot down. She had been patient, hoping Mrs. Marshall would get tired of being so ''helpful'' or Brian would reach his saturation point and tell her to stop, but apparently neither was going to happen on its own.

Her internal fuming reached a boiling point as a sleek red Ferrari pulled into the dirt drive and parked next to Mr. Stevens's company truck. It looked like Mrs. Marshall's ''gift'' was going to be even more costly than she'd feared.

The man drove a Ferrari! Mrs. Marshall had described him as up and coming, specializing in commercial construction but designing a few houses on the side. She'd made it sound as if it would be a real feather in this guy's cap to design a house for San Diego's star pitcher, Brian Marshall. One more feather and he could reconstruct an ostrich!

The sun hit the windshield of the sports car, preventing her from getting a glimpse of architecture's Boy Wonder. The door opened with a soft click and her conviction that his fee would be high was reinforced as she saw his polished leather shoes—handmade, probably Gucci, she guessed. As he closed the door and turned to walk toward them, Melissa slowly moved her eyes up his body, taking in the impeccably tailored suit. The back of her neck began to tingle and an unsettling awareness of the man within the suit swept over her.

She had the impression of handsome features and dark hair before Brian's hand on her arm drew her attention. ''I've decided what you can get me for

Christmas," he quipped for her ears only, his eyes glued to the Ferrari.

She looked back at the approaching architect. Surely she was seeing things. Thick black hair and strong ruggedly handsome features didn't prove anything—southern California was full of gorgeous, tall, dark-haired men, but when he stopped in front of them and removed his sunglasses to reveal familiar deep-blue eyes, all doubt was swept from her mind.

"Mr. Edwards, good to be working with you again," Mr. Stevens said.

Melissa was vaguely aware of Mr. Stevens making introductions. Morgan shook hands with Brian. He took her hand next. "Nice to meet you," he said politely. He started to withdraw his hand and turn away, but then he was facing her again. A warm smile took the place of his polite, businessman façade. "Melly?"

He looked older; after all, it had been ten years. But the changes were subtle, added strength, maturity, and the confidence that comes with success. He looked wonderful!

"Hello, Morgan," she managed to say, despite the shock of seeing him again.

"You two know each other? Why didn't you tell me?" Brian's voice was laced with subtle undertones Melissa had come to recognize as meaning he was less than pleased with a situation.

"Morgan and Lucas used to be best friends, but it's been years since I've seen him. I had no idea that *this* Mr. Edwards was Morgan. I didn't even know he was an architect." She realized how little she'd known about Morgan. He'd been there in her dreams and fantasies, but she hadn't even known what he'd majored in.

"Lucas was a good friend, we shared an apartment while we were going to UCSD, but when I went to Georgia for graduate school we lost contact," Morgan explained to Brian before turning back to Melissa. "So, what's Luc up to these days?" he asked.

"He's running the sporting goods stores."

"Your dad retire?"

"From the business end of things. He still works with the customers. That's always been his favorite part of it."

"Are you working for the family business, too?"

"Yes, I handle the advertising, publicity, and assorted odds and ends." It had been her idea to have the autograph day where she'd met Brian. "You can usually catch Lucas at the original Mission Bay store on Mondays and Fridays. It's next to impossible to reach him at his home."

"He must not be married," Morgan said.

Was *Morgan* married? Melissa nonchalantly glanced at his left hand. He wasn't wearing a ring. Of course that didn't prove anything. Not all men wore wedding rings. She hoped he wasn't married. Good grief, what was she thinking? *She* was engaged. What difference would his marital status make? Come on, Melissa, get a grip on yourself.

She couldn't seem to tear her eyes from Morgan. She had seen his face so many times in her dreams at night and her fantasies during the day. The crush she'd had on him, yes, she admitted now it was just a crush, had lingered several more years after the Valentine incident. As her awareness of male/female relationships had grown, she had visualized the two of them in a wide variety of romantic situations. She had even imagined a wedding and a very vivid, if youthfully naive, honeymoon.

She shifted uncomfortably, grateful no one could read her thoughts.

"How does that sound to you, honey?"

Brian's question pulled her attention back to the three men and the matter at hand. She wasn't sure what Brian was referring to, but she trusted his judgment. "Whatever you think best." She couldn't believe she'd said something so trite and submissive, even to avoid admitting she hadn't been listening by asking him to repeat the question.

She glanced at Morgan out of the corner of her eye. The subtle lifting of one eyebrow registered his puzzlement at her acquiesence.

Brian took her hand, and the four of them walked over the lot. Morgan occasionally made a note in a small leather notebook.

"Do you have someone for the landscaping yet?" Morgan asked.

"Mother has contacted someone," Brian assured him.

Morgan nodded and looked down, but not before Melissa saw the left side of his mouth quirk slightly.

"I'll need their name and number so I can confer with them. I'd like to have final approval on their designs before they do any planting."

"No problem," Brian assured him.

"Do you have an interior designer?"

"Not yet," Brian answered.

Morgan reached into the back pocket of his note-book and pulled out several business cards. He handed them to Brian. "These are three local interior designers. I've worked with each of them before. They're all very good."

Brian handed the cards to Melissa. "Why don't you set up appointments with all three and see whose style you like best." He smiled down at her. "Be sure to take Mother with you."

Morgan's professional manners never slipped, but Melissa could see the scorn in his eyes and feel his disdain. "I'd like to get a feel for what you need from the interior."

"What we need from the interior?" Brian asked.

"Number of bedrooms, bathrooms, do you need a home office, a large room for parties, size of the kitchen. I imagine with your line of work, you'll want a gym room?"

"Near the pool, if possible," Brian said.

Morgan reached into his jacket pocket and pulled out an envelope. "I have a list of items here if you'd like to go over it at your leisure. Be sure to write down that you'd like the gym by the pool. Also, if you could pay attention to how much time you spend in each room of your house or apartment. What time of day each room gets the most use." He handed the envelope to Brian.

"What's the reason for that?" Melissa asked.

"I like my buildings to make maximum use of the

natural lighting, so I put the rooms you will be using most in the morning on the east side of the house and the late-afternoon rooms on the west."

"Ecologically designed to save natural resources— I like the idea." Brian turned to Melissa. "Honey, remember to work that into an interview."

"I'd like to do a three-wing split-level," Morgan continued, ignoring Brian's remarks.

"What did Mother think?" Brian asked.

"Mrs. Marshall suggested two stories, but I think a traditional two-story would be too overpowering for this lot. A split-level would blend into the surroundings much more effectively. I have several ideas for possible exterior designs."

"Which did Mother like?"

"Mrs. Marshall and I didn't discuss them." Melissa could hear a subtle coolness in Morgan's reply.

Where did he get off judging Brian? Granted Brian was overdoing the concern for his mother's opinion, but she *was* paying the designing fees.

"Are you planning to go with solar energy?" He paused briefly, but not long enough for Brian to ask about *Mother*. "Mrs. Marshall liked the idea."

Morgan looked at Melissa, as if waiting for her to speak up. So, he was going to judge her, too?

"Solar energy sounds fine," she replied, her voice cool.

"I'll have some exterior sketches ready by next Tuesday. Would it be convenient for you to come by my office around one?"

Brian answered, "Tuesday, one o'clock, sounds fine."

He didn't check with Melissa, but she shouldn't have any trouble getting off work. She was just grateful that he didn't bring up his mother again. Morgan's last reference to Mrs. Marshall must have sunk in.

They started walking back to the vehicles.

"Mr. Stevens," Brian said. "I almost forgot. I've got the baseball for your grandson in the car." He picked up the pace, Mr. Stevens following him.

Morgan fell back, gently taking hold of Melissa's upper arm to keep her with him.

"So, when's the wedding?"

"The second Saturday in January."

"Ah, that's why there's such a rush on this job." He released her arm, but the warm tingling his touch had set off remained. "How long have you known this guy?" He nodded toward Brian.

Why was he asking and what business was it of his? Melissa wondered. But she answered him anyway. "Three months."

"Three months? During baseball season?"

"Yes." Melissa looked up at him, her eyes narrowing. "Is there a problem with that?"

"You can't have spent much time together, with the team practicing, personal appearances, and games, especially the out-of-town games. How well do you know this guy, Melly?"

"It's Melissa or Lissa. No one calls me Melly anymore."

His gaze swept over her face, lingering a moment

too long on her lips. His eyes flashed, as the corners of his mouth turned upward. "No one but me." His voice flowed over her, sending shivers down to her toes. "You didn't answer my question."

Blast it all! It was none of his business. He had no right to ask such personal questions. And he had no business looking at her that way, calling her by a nickname she'd abandoned years ago, making her feel fourteen years old again. "Do you give all your clients the third degree?"

Morgan took a step away from her, his back stiffening. "Guess I overstepped my boundaries. Sorry, it won't happen again."

He turned and started toward where Brian and Mr. Stevens stood talking. Melissa followed.

"Ready to go, Lissa?" Brian asked as she reached him.

She nodded.

Seated next to Brian, Melissa wished his car didn't have bucket seats. She needed to be close to him. Although she hadn't let on, Morgan's questions had unsettled her. How well did she know Brian? They really *hadn't* spent much time together. Were they rushing things?

"Lissa, are you all right?"

Brian's voice interrupted Melissa's thoughts. She smiled at him. "Guess I'm a little tired." She looked around. They were already several blocks from the lot.

"I was suggesting that we invite Mother to go with us next Tuesday when we meet Mr. Edwards to see the plans."

It was the perfect opening to let Brian know how frustrated she was with his mother's continual interference, but she let it pass. She didn't want an argument. She needed to feel at peace with him, to feel the rightness of her decision to marry him.

Mrs. Marshall would be going back to Chicago after the wedding. She could put up with her that long. What worried her most at the moment was the small, uneasy feeling stirring in the pit of her stomach and the image of a man with dark hair, blue eyes, and a slow, sexy smile that refused to fade from her mind.

He'd been right, she was a beautiful woman. He could almost see her peeking out the window of the sketch he was working on.

Unfortunately, it seemed that her personality had changed. She'd been a sweet, sensitive kid, but today when he questioned her, she'd been almost hostile. And he certainly had never figured her for a yes-dear-whatever-you-say-dear type.

It really wasn't any of his business. But there was something about Marshall that he didn't like. He could see how a woman might find him attractive, and he pitched a helluva baseball game. Somehow he'd never pictured Melly as the type who would fall for a jock. Especially one who was still firmly attached to his mother's apron strings—though he sincerely doubted Beverly Marshall had ever even owned an apron. With her smartly styled light-blond hair, flawless makeup, and miniskirt, she didn't look old enough to have a son playing major-league ball.

He'd told her so last night when they'd looked at the site.

She seemed nice enough, but he suspected all Brian's concern for his mother's thoughts and opinions couldn't be one-sided. She must be partially responsible for it.

He put his pencil in the brass pencil holder on his desk and stretched. He would work more on the plans tomorrow. He had until Tuesday to finish them.

He hoped Melly knew what she was getting herself into. But then again, what difference did it make to him? His job was to design their house. He never worried about any of his other clients. Of course, none of his other clients had had a crush on him in the past.

It was in the past, ten years past. He had known it was just a crush. He had told her she would find someone of her own one day and wouldn't give an old fossil like him the time of day.

His mind flashed a picture of her. She'd looked properly professional in the black skirt and jacket she'd had on that morning, jacket parting as she'd walked to show emerald-green silk. She'd certainly filled out. Physical desire shot through him. He shifted, trying to get comfortable in his blue jeans. He didn't feel like an old fossil, damn it!

Three months . . . she'd met Brian Marshall three months ago. Part of him couldn't help wondering what would have happened if he'd walked back into her life first?

TWO

"Lissa, set an extra place at the table. Lucas called earlier and said he was bringing a guest with him," her mother, Jean, said as she popped her head into the dining room.

Whenever possible, the Ellison family got together for Sunday dinner. Since their engagement, Brian had been accompanying Melissa, and since her arrival Beverly had been included. Lucas, on the other hand, always came alone.

"Do you think he's finally getting ready to settle down?" Melissa turned to her mother.

"I have no idea. Has he been seeing anyone special lately?"

"Actually, Mom, Luc and I rarely discuss our private lives. But this is the first time he's brought a woman home for Sunday dinner. Could be significant."

"Well, I must say it's about time."

Melissa chuckled. "Worried about grandchildren to carry the Ellison name?" she teased.

"Is there anything I can help with?" Beverly Marshall asked as she entered the dining room. She brushed at her sleeve, the fuchsia color of her perfectly manicured nails an exact match for her silk dress. She came every week dressed to the teeth, although she'd been told casual was the order of the day at the Ellison's. Brian always complied. He and Melissa were wearing matching Conquistador sweatsuits in red and gold.

"Dinner's under control, thanks. You can help Lissa set the table if you'd like," Jean answered before disappearing back into the kitchen.

Melissa's mind was only half on the task at hand. She was trying to remember if Lucas had mentioned any particular woman lately. He always seemed to be dating someone, but never stayed with one woman long. Could he really be getting serious about someone at last?

"This is such a nice tradition," Beverly remarked as she walked around the table, every now and then moving a piece of silverware or napkin a fraction of an inch away from where Melissa'd placed it. "When you and Brian move to Chicago, we'll have Sunday dinner at my house each week. After he retires, of course."

"Perhaps." Melissa managed to smile. What a nightmare of an idea! Nothing against Chicago, of course, but she had no desire to live within a thousand miles of Beverly. She and Brian had discussed his future plans to go into sports broadcasting when he retired from the team. But she had assumed he would stick with the Conquistadors, and they would still live in San Diego—well, just above San Diego; they were having their house built in La Jolla. She realized now that she would have to discuss it with him . . . soon.

"We're here!" Lucas bellowed as he threw open the front door.

"We'll have to talk to him about the proper way to impress a date." Jean shook her head as she came through the dining room on her way to the front door.

"Good heavens! Frank, come and see who Luc's brought." Jean's excited yell sent Melissa running to the front door. Beverly followed at a slower pace.

Standing in the entry hall with Lucas was Morgan, and Jean and Frank Ellison were welcoming him to Sunday dinner with as much enthusiasm as if he were their own son. There had been times during his earlier friendship with Lucas when it had seemed like he was.

"We thought you were bringing a date." Melissa walked over to her brother, who was watching the scene and looking very pleased with himself.

"Just because you're ready to settle down, don't try to clip my wings." Lucas was six feet of ruggedly masculine charm with the same blond hair and green eyes his sister had.

Brian entered from the family room. Melissa noticed that he seemed surprised to see Morgan and less than pleased. She didn't have time to analyze why as just then the oven buzzer went off.

Melissa ran into the kitchen. She was glad for an excuse to get away. Her heart was racing overtime and her toes were curling just from looking at Morgan. She could close her eyes and see him clearly—snug-fitting blue jeans, knitted ski sweater in shades of blue. *Drat,* why was this happening now?

She managed to get through dinner appearing normal as Morgan and Lucas monopolized most of the conversation, filling each other in on the last ten years. Frank asked after Morgan's parents and found that they were well and had retired to Palm Springs. Beverly managed to get her two cents in at every turn, always knowing someone important in every city mentioned.

When Jean asked Morgan over coffee if he was married, Melissa almost dropped her cup.

"No, I'm not," Morgan answered the question, after a brief glance at Melissa's cup now sitting on her saucer. Only the rocking of the liquid was left to indicate what a close call it had been.

"You're as bad as Lucas," Jean chided. "What's your excuse?"

"I'm rarely in one place long enough to develop a serious relationship."

"Some excuse," Melissa surprised herself by speaking. "Haven't you ever heard of love at first sight?"

"Sure, but it takes more than chemistry to make a successful marriage. Too many couples rush to the altar. If they'd slow down and get to know each other better first, it would prevent a lot of divorces."

Morgan kept his eyes on her as he took a sip of his coffee.

Morgan's words sounded very universal and general in scope, but Melissa knew the message behind them had been aimed specifically at her and Brian. She had to bite her tongue to still the angry reply bubbling within her. But she couldn't control the anger that flared up in her eyes to meet the challenge glaring in his.

"Don't mind her, Morgan. You know lovebirds. They always want to see everybody else as tied down as they are," Lucas said, breaking the tension.

Melissa looked away from Morgan. Brian, who'd been very quiet during dinner, took her hand under the table, giving it a supportive squeeze.

Her mind was in a whirl. Morgan's remarks had made her angry. On the other hand, six months ago she would have readily agreed with him. When had her views changed? When she'd met Brian? He'd swept her off her feet. Had she jumped into this engagement too quickly?

With all hands pitching in, except Beverly's, it took little time for the table to be cleared and everything stacked in the kitchen.

"Hey, you still have the volleyball net," Morgan remarked, glancing out the kitchen window into the backyard.

"The poles are the same, but the net has been replaced several times. You've been away a long time, pal." Lucas opened the sliding-glass door and headed out to the patio. "It's not too cold out here. Anyone feel like a game?"

Frank brought the volleyball out of the garage, and teams were formed. Morgan, Luc, and Jean against Melissa, Brian, and Frank. Beverly was appointed referee since she was wearing a dress. She muttered a few words about her manicure.

The game moved at a brisk pace. Both teams scored equally for a while, until Melissa had a run of bad luck. Tripping over a sprinkler head, she sent the ball into the net. Getting a charley horse in her wrist just as the ball got to her, she awkwardly hit a pass to Brian and the ball fell short. During the next play she was running backward to make a hit, determined not to blow this shot, and plowed right into Brian.

He moved her roughly away from him. "What do you think you're doing? That was my ball. Didn't you hear me call it?"

She'd been concentrating so hard on watching the ball, she hadn't been listening. "No. I didn't hear you. Would I have been trying to get it if I had? Last thing I heard, I was supposed to set it up for you to spike. When did the plan change?"

"When you started playing fumbleball! You realize, don't you, that just one more foul-up on your part and we forfeit this game."

"*Game*, Brian, that's right—this is just a game. We're supposed to be having fun here. It doesn't matter who wins." Melissa placed clenched fists on her hips.

Brian retrieved the ball and pitched it over the net for Morgan to serve. Morgan coldly nodded his thanks and served the ball. It sailed straight for

Melissa. She fully intended to set it up neatly for Brian, but the extra adrenaline caused by her anger sent the ball flying over his head.

Morgan and Luc let out a victory yell that prevented Melissa from hearing whatever Brian mumbled under his breath. The two friends continued their celebrating with a high-five fest.

Brian turned to Melissa, "It's time we left."

Melissa looked at her watch. It was only seven-thirty. They usually stayed at least until nine o'clock. "But it's still early."

"I'm leaving." His voice was tight. "Are you coming with me?"

"Brian, what's with you all of a sudden?" Melissa noticed the celebration on the other side of the net had settled down and that everyone was watching the two of them.

"Are you coming with me?" Brian repeated.

She could feel the tension in the air. Brian waited for her answer, daring her to defy him. Beverly nervously adjusted her dress over her knees. Her mother and father watched supportively. Morgan, tense and angry, looked ready to barge through the net. Lucas's restraining hand on his shoulder showing he'd started to do just that.

It was still early, and she refused to be dragged home like a child who had misbehaved. She was not a child, and she'd done nothing wrong. She hadn't thrown the game intentionally. The mishaps had all been accidental.

Melissa took a deep breath. "No." She pulled her

shoulders back. "I always help Mom clean up the kitchen."

Jean came around the net. "Honey, you don't have to stay just for that. I'll put Luc to work."

Melissa looked up at Brian. The unaccustomed coldness in his eyes and the stubborn set of his jaw decided her. "I'm going to help with the kitchen. If you can't wait, I'll catch a ride home with Luc." Without waiting for his reply, she headed into the house.

She was loading dishes into the dishwasher when she heard the front door open and close, followed by the sound of Brian's car driving away.

Jean came into the kitchen and began working silently alongside her daughter. When the job was finished she asked, "Would you like a cup of herbal tea?"

"No thanks, Mom."

"Do you want to stay out here and talk a bit?"

Melissa shook her head. "There's nothing to talk about."

"All right, but keep in mind that things are always tense when weddings are being planned. You've heard of prenuptial jitters. I'm sure that's all this is."

"I hope so." If his behavior this evening was a permanent part of Brian's personality, she wasn't sure she could live with it. "We haven't had much time together, though." Melissa was surprised to hear Morgan's words coming out of her own mouth.

"True, but I only knew your father two weeks before we were married."

"Did you argue at all before the wedding?"

Jean laughed. "Did we ever! The last forty-eight hours before the ceremony, I almost called it off several times." She gave her daughter a hug. "Just listen to your heart, honey."

Listen to her heart. It was wonderful advice. The only problem was, at the moment, her heart seemed to be speaking in a foreign language.

"So tell me is the Mighty Marshall always such a poor sport?" Morgan asked Luc. The two of them were looking at old photos in what had once been Luc's room.

"I don't know. This is the first time we've played a game together. He was really ticked off about losing."

"Sure was." Morgan nodded.

"Must have been hard on his hot-shot jock image to lose to a couple of old guys and a mom."

Morgan responded with a half laugh, before turning serious. "I hope Melly knows what she's doing."

Luc looked speculatively at Morgan. "For a minute there, I thought you were going to go right through the net and deck the guy."

"Well, her big brother didn't seem to be making any moves to help." Morgan tried to sidetrack the suspicions he could almost sense building in Luc's mind, suspicions he didn't want to admit even to himself. He *had* wanted to deck the guy. Deck him and teach him a few things about how to treat Melly. It wasn't so unusual for him to want to rescue a lady in distress, but the strong urge for a physical encounter surprised him.

"She was doing just fine on her own. If she'd needed my help she would have asked and I'd have been there for her."

Morgan closed the photo album he'd been holding and placed it back on the shelf.

Luc followed suit. "I used to think she had a thing for you."

"Me?"

"You! She used to watch you like a hawk when you were here, and your picture disappeared out of my senior yearbook."

"Are you sure you didn't cut it out to use on your dart board?"

"Why would I do that?"

"Because I took Gail Farmer to the senior prom."

"Gail Farmer . . ." He grinned. "I'd forgotten all about her. Wonder what she's been up to?"

"Probably married."

"You're right." Luc sighed. "How long do you think you'll be in town?"

"A while. Besides the Marshall house, I'm working on an office building downtown and a minimall in Chula Vista."

"Great. Why don't I see what I can do about locating some of the old gang and having a party?"

"Wait until next year and it will be time for our fifteen-year class reunion."

"Don't say that. It makes me feel so old."

Morgan laughed. "How old is Marshall?"

"Brian or Beverly?"

"Brian."

"Somewhere around twenty-four or twenty-five, I guess."

"He is a youngster, isn't he?" *Young, yes, but just the right age for Melly, damn it.*

"It was just a guess. If you really need to know, we can buy his baseball card and find out," Luc joked.

"Don't tell me you still collect baseball cards?" Morgan said.

Luc pulled open his desk drawer and took out an old cigar box. "I haven't added to the collection in years, but I haven't got rid of these. Guess I keep thinking maybe someday I'll have a son to pass them on to. But since I need to get married first—"

"Mine are in my parents' attic, for the same reason." Morgan took the box Luc held out to him. He opened the lid, picked up a few cards, and wistfully shuffled through them. "Came damn close once."

"Really? Me, too."

For a moment they stood quietly, each reliving the pain of lost love.

"No way—" Morgan broke the tense silence. "Love-em-and-Leave-em Luc would never settle for one chick with so many to choose from."

"And Electrifying Edwards would never deprive the masses of his expertise by limiting himself to a single person-of-the-female-persuasion."

Morgan put the cards back into the box, closed the lid, and handed it to Luc. Luc put the box into the desk and closed the drawer. The baseball cards were safely tucked away, and their brief moment of mutual vulnerability was safely tucked away with them.

Melissa, Luc, and Morgan arrived in the parking lot of her apartment building at the same time as her roommate, Carol. Still the nonstop bundle of energy she'd been in junior high, Carol lured the men into the apartment with the promise of cheesecake.

"So you're not living with Marshall?" Luc and Carol were far enough ahead that they didn't hear Morgan's question.

"No."

"Isn't that a little unusual for engaged couples these days?" He sounded amused, self-satisfied.

"Many couples do live together before marriage, but not *all*."

"Guess it would be a bit awkward with 'Mother' living in, too."

Melissa ground her teeth at Morgan's perfect imitation of Brian. Once again he was treading on sensitive areas that weren't any of his business. Worse— he knew it, but still persisted.

"Will you two hurry up?" Carol called to them from the open door of the apartment.

They picked up their pace and were soon in the apartment.

"Nice," Morgan remarked, looking around the homey country living room that Melissa and Carol had decorated themselves.

"Too frilly," Luc gave his opinion as he pushed several calico throw pillows out of his way before sitting down on the couch.

Morgan sat down in the rocking chair across from Luc.

"I'll go help Carol with the cheesecake. Anyone want coffee or tea?"

"Coffee," Luc answered.

"Morgan?"

"That's fine with me, too."

"Lissa," Carol called from the kitchen. "The answering machine is blinking."

"I'll be right there."

Morgan flashed her a wicked smile. "Must be the glory boy calling to apologize."

She heard Luc give a low whistle as she stormed from the room.

There were several messages on the machine, and one of the messages for her *was* Brian.

"Is everything okay, Lissa?" Carol asked. "You left here with Brian, but Luc brings you home, and who's this Morgan guy? He looks familiar. Why does Brian want you to call him as soon as you get in?"

"I'll answer all your questions later, preferably one at a time." Melissa started fixing the coffee while Carol took care of the cheesecake.

Melissa thought about calling Brian while she waited for the coffee to brew, but decided to wait until Luc and Morgan left. She told herself she was just being a good hostess, but in the back of her mind she knew she didn't want to talk to Brian with Morgan there. She didn't want to give him any more fuel for his cutting remarks.

Good thing he was hostile, though. If he wasn't,

she would have a real problem on her hands with the strange way her body reacted when she was near him.

When the coffee was ready she took four mugs full into the living room. Luckily, Carol's bubbly personality kept the conversational ball rolling. She was very interested in Morgan's work and the fact that he was designing Melissa's future home.

Melissa was only half listening. Her eyes kept returning to Morgan, taking in every detail of him.

She was sure if she looked down at her chest she would see the outline of her heart as it beat double-time within her. She slipped out of her favorite comfy tennis shoes that now felt too tight and crossed and recrossed her legs, trying in vain to ease the ache spreading through her lower body.

Melissa felt a strong surge of gratitude for her brother when Luc announced that since tomorrow was a workday, they'd better be on their way.

"I'll see you Tuesday afternoon," Morgan said to Melissa as the four of them stood at the door.

After a few seconds of stunned silence, Melissa remembered their appointment. "Yes, of course. Brian and I will be there at one." She didn't dare mention that Beverly would be with them.

The minute the door closed behind the men, Carol turned to Melissa and demanded, "All right, fill me in." She plunked herself down on one end of the couch, pulling a throw pillow in her lap.

Melissa sat down in the rocking chair and regretted it the minute she felt Morgan's body heat on the cushions. "Have you ever felt your heartbeat race, had your toes curl, and felt a heavy ache in your lower abdominal regions just from looking at a man?''

Carol laughed triumphantly. ''I told you that you guys wouldn't be able to keep to your plan of waiting until after the wedding. Listen, if you and Brian want to borrow the apartment some night—''

''Carol,'' Melissa cut her friend off. She took a deep breath and closed her eyes. ''It's not Brian,'' she said softly.

At no other time in their long friendship had Melissa ever seen Carol at a loss for words.

''Not Brian?'' she managed to stammer after several minutes of silence.

Melissa shook her head. ''And that's only part of the problem.'' She told Carol about Brian's behavior during the volleyball game and her mother's opinion that it was just prenuptial jitters.

''It might be prenuptial jitters on *his* part, but I don't think that explains what you're feeling for this other guy. Who is he, by the way?''

''Morgan.''

''Luc's friend? Will you be seeing much of him?''

''He's designing our house. How can I avoid it?''

Carol hit her forehead with the palm of her hand. ''That's right! How could I have forgotten? When did these feelings start?''

''The minute I saw him again.''

''Again?''

Melissa refreshed Carol's memory about the picture in the diary, the Valentine, and the Valentine's Day trip to McCoy's.

"I knew he looked familiar! He was your first boyfriend. You never did tell me the details of your breaking up."

"Because there weren't any details to tell." Melissa explained about the mixup.

Carol whistled. "You must have hated me for putting you in a fix like that."

"Not at all. I was angry at myself for not having told the truth about Morgan from the beginning. I had no one but me to blame."

They sat in silence for a while. Then Melissa continued. "I used to dream about him all the time and create fantasies about the two of us together." She rocked slowly back and forth in the chair. "Do you remember the last two weeks of Miss Mayhew's science class in ninth grade?"

"Who could forget it? That was the most graphic sexed we'd ever had and the first time we'd had it co-ed."

"Well . . . when she would talk about 'the male partner' and 'the female partner,' I would picture Morgan and me . . ." She stopped rocking. "Do you think seeing Morgan has made my body remember feelings from back then? Awakening desire, the glow of being in love with love for the first time?"

"What you describe sounds like a good healthy case of desire. Don't you feel the same thing with Brian? I think you should if you're going to marry him!"

"It's hard to explain. It's different with Brian. I'm looking forward to the honeymoon, but I don't mind waiting."

"Does necking with him leave you all hot and bothered?"

Melissa laughed. "You're the only person I know that still calls it necking."

"And you're the only engaged person I know who's not doing anything else," Carol threw back. "You didn't answer my question."

"Yes . . . necking with Brian leaves me all hot and bothered, but it fades away quickly once he leaves. I have control over my body with Brian. But when I'm around Morgan there's no controlling my reactions."

"Heavens, Lissa. What are you going to do?"

"I don't know." The telephone rang. "But for starters, I'll get the phone."

As she suspected, it was Brian. He was contrite and apologetic.

"Mother says it's normal for engaged couples to go through this," he said.

"My mom said pretty much the same thing. What do you think?"

"I guess they're probably right."

"Would it be easier . . . less tension on us if . . . um . . . if maybe we were sleeping together?" Melissa shocked herself with the question. Would sleeping with Brian change what she was feeling for Morgan? She didn't think so, but would marrying Brian have any effect, either?

Brian cleared his throat. "No, I think our original decision to wait was a good one. We'll be married soon and this will all be behind us. Everything will be all right, honey, you'll see."

They said their good-byes. Melissa stood for a few moments with her hand on the phone, wondering if they would be getting married as planned. Would everything really be all right?

THREE

Things were even farther from all right Tuesday afternoon at three o'clock as Melissa, Brian, and Beverly were driving to Melissa's apartment. The meeting with Morgan had gone smoothly enough, but now Beverly was sitting in the backseat making a list of changes and additional features that she planned to call Morgan about.

"Are you *sure* you want the morning sun coming right in the bedroom window? You could move the bathroom to the east wall."

Brian grunted noncommittally, his attention totally focused on the steadily increasing afternoon traffic.

Melissa looked over her shoulder to see Beverly scribbling rapidly in her ever-present notebook. "Bev, why don't you make your list and then Brian and I will go over it with you? If we decide to make any of the suggested changes, *we* will contact Morgan."

"Well, I didn't have anything else planned for this afternoon or evening . . . what with Brian flying up to San Francisco with the team. I've got plenty of time to handle it."

"Actually, I wasn't thinking about the time aspect." Melissa turned to Brian. "Brian, don't you think we should approve any suggested changes before Morgan is called?" *Who's going to be living in this house?* she longed to ask him.

"Yes, dear." He didn't sound very convinced. "Mother, make your list but don't do any more than that until Lissa and I have a chance to go over it with you. All right?"

Beverly didn't answer, but Brian didn't seem to notice as he pulled up in front of Melissa's apartment complex. "You've got the phone number of the hotel. Call me if you need anything, honey." He leaned over and kissed her briefly. "I'll see you Thursday."

Melissa bit her bottom lip, trying to decide whether to mention Beverly's lack of response to his request. Brian mistook her hesitation and pulled her into his arms. "It's only two days, Lissa. And after we're married, you'll be able to make these publicity trips with me."

Melissa sighed as she returned his hug. Once she was out of the car, Beverly moved up into the front seat. As they drove away, Melissa thought she saw Beverly pick up Brian's phone receiver.

She wouldn't dare. She must be calling someone else. Surely Brian wouldn't let her call Morgan.

Despite her certainty, she found herself dialing Morgan's office the minute she got into the apartment.

Morgan's answering machine told her the line was busy, but she should stay on the line and all calls would be forwarded in order. Busy . . . but that didn't prove anything, did it? He could be talking to someone else.

Fifteen minutes later she tried Brian's car and Morgan's office. They were both busy. Still not conclusive proof, but this was going to be her house and she was not going to take the chance of Beverly making changes behind her back. If she wasn't on the phone to Morgan now, Melissa was sure she would be sometime before Brian came home.

Enough was enough. She thought about changing out of the gray wool suit she'd worn to the meeting, but decided against wasting the extra time. She dug her car keys out of her purse and set off. She knew she would have to face some mocking comments from Morgan, but it was better than being stuck in a house she was unhappy with.

Taking surface roads, to avoid the freeway traffic, she headed back downtown. She hoped Morgan would still be at the office when she got there. The sky darkened as the afternoon clouds thickened.

A few drops splattered against her windshield just before she pulled into the garage parking on the lower levels of the multileveled skyscraper where Morgan had his office. There was a line of cars making their way out of the parking lot. Once again Melissa hoped Morgan hadn't left. Maybe she should have waited until his phone line was clear, but if it was Beverly on the other end that could have taken hours. Maybe she should have gotten his home number from Lucas and called him later.

She hadn't thought of these things before and now that she was already here, she might as well go up and see if she'd missed him or not.

Going against the flow of traffic, she made her way to the elevators and up to the tenth floor. As she'd feared, Morgan's door was locked when she tried it, the reception area dark and empty.

Drat, why had she been so impatient? Now she was going to have to fight the work traffic which was always a misery, but would be even worse if the raindrops had developed into something. She started to turn away, but then noticed a strip of light showing beneath the double wooden doors of his inner office. She crossed her fingers and knocked loudly on the outer glass door.

The double doors opened, spilling light into the reception area. Morgan came toward her slowly. With the light behind him, she was unable to read his expression. He unlocked the door and opened it for her.

"Forget something, Melly?"

"No. I'd like to talk to you . . . if you have a few minutes."

He looked down at her silently.

She noticed that his hair was rumpled, his jacket was off, his tie gone, and his shirt partially unbuttoned. Did he have a woman waiting for him in the other room? "That is, if it's convenient."

Still he said nothing.

"Listen, I'll call your secretary in the morning and make an appointment." His secretary! Was he having an affair with his secretary? Right here in the office? A strong reaction shot through her. Jealousy—although she'd never admit it.

As Melissa started to back up, Morgan reached out and took hold of her upper arm. "Now is fine." He gently pulled her in, locked the door behind them, and started back toward the double doors.

As they entered his office, Melissa looked around it and through the glass to his workroom. If there'd been a woman here, she'd slipped out the back way. Her eyes drifted over to Morgan's jacket and tie lying on the couch in his workroom. He let go of her arm to close the double doors. Melissa glanced behind them.

"Looking for someone?"

She started to deny it, but his short laugh cut her off. Guess she had been rather obvious. She gestured to the front of his unbuttoned shirt. His tanned chest looked rock-hard beneath its mat of black hair. She longed to touch it and see if it was as hard as it looked. She swallowed. "I thought maybe I was interrupting something." She looked up to meet his amused gaze.

"My shower."

"Shower?"

"I was getting ready to take a shower. When I work late in the evenings, I usually change into something more comfortable once the front office is closed."

"You have a shower here?"

"Won't believe it until you see it? This way, please." He led her across the office and into his workroom. A large drafting table and a desk full of computer equipment sat facing the window. Morgan opened one of two doors against the far wall. Sure enough, it was a bathroom complete with closet by the door and shower stall at the far end. "Convinced?"

Melissa was angry at herself—both for caring whether he'd been in a hot and heavy clinch with a woman and for letting him see what she'd suspected and that she cared. She walked back into the workroom. The outer wall was window from floor to ceiling and she could see it was now raining in earnest. The beautiful view of the bay that she'd admired earlier in the day was now dismal and gray, the palm trees bending in the wind.

"So, can I get you something to drink?" Morgan asked.

"No thanks."

"Why don't you have a seat and tell me what brought you all the way back over here."

Melissa sat down on one end of the couch. Morgan picked up his jacket and tie and hung them in the closet.

"I'd like to ask for a favor . . . ." Melissa began, once Morgan was seated on the opposite end of the couch. "I have a feeling Beverly Marshall will be calling you in the near future."

"She's already called." He stretched his arm across the back of the couch, the motion spreading the gap in his shirt wider.

Melissa pressed her lips tightly together and silently

counted to ten. "When your phone was busy, I thought she might have."

"She did, and she's full of new ideas."

Melissa groaned. "Such as?"

"For starters she wants the master bathroom moved to the east side of the bedroom, she wants to change the bay window in the hallway next to the dining room into an extra closet for your table linens . . ." His voice trailed off. "Do I need to go on?"

"No, I get the picture."

"I can't help wonder whose house this is going to be?"

She'd wondered the same thing herself, so her reply was prickly and defensive. "Mine and Brian's."

Morgan shrugged his shoulders and shook his head. "Is Beverly going to be living with you?"

"No. She's going back to Chicago." She'd better not change her plans and decide to move in with them, Melissa thought.

"Then why are you letting her run this whole show?"

"I'm not! That's why I'm here."

"Does she know you're here?"

"No."

"Does Marshall know you're here?"

"No." She shifted uncomfortably, wishing he would button his shirt.

"Does he know his mother was calling me?"

"I'm not sure. He told her to wait until the two of us had a chance to go over the list with her, but she picked up the phone the minute I was out of the car. He might not have been listening, though. He has an uncanny ability to completely tune her out when he wants to."

"He didn't tune her out when you were here. He asked her opinion on everything." There was no mistaking the scorn in his voice.

"Well, she *is* paying the designing fees!"

"My designing fees?"

"Yes."

"Why? Don't try to tell me that the Mighty Marshall can't afford my fees. The amount of his latest contract settlement was all over the news."

Melissa sighed. "It was Beverly's idea of a wedding gift."

"What happened to the traditional toaster?"

"I don't know, but I would really appreciate it if you wouldn't change anything on the house on Beverly's say-so."

"What about Brian's?" he asked softly.

Melissa closed her eyes. Surely Brian wouldn't make any major changes to the house without consulting her first. But then she'd been sure he wouldn't have let Beverly call Morgan from the car phone, either, and it appeared that he had. She opened her eyes and looked at Morgan. "Not without checking with me first, please."

"At least you're standing up for your rights. But wouldn't it be better in the long run if you confronted the two of them directly?"

"I did mention it in the car. Brian was a bit preoccupied and Beverly obviously didn't pay any attention."

"Then you'd better try again!" He ran his hands

through his hair in frustration. "I can keep them from changing the floor plan, and I have some pull with the landscaping and the interior design. But will it stop with the plans for the house or will Beverly Marshall be running your whole life?"

"No," she told him, but her eyes told him he'd hit a vulnerable nerve.

"What's to stop her?"

"Me!"

"How? By asking everyone for favors?" He leaned toward her. "Melly, you can't spend your whole life sneaking around behind the scenes to make sure you don't get walked on at every turn."

"It won't be like that." It was hard for her to meet his gaze—those blue eyes she had fantasized about so many times. But dropping her gaze was even more disconcerting since his bare chest had been part of her fantasies, too. "When Brian gets back from San Francisco, we'll have time to talk it over."

"What's to talk over? The man is already putting his mother's needs and opinions over those of his future wife. And if you think that will change once you're married, you're fooling yourself."

"You don't know that for certain," she told him angrily.

"A marriage is supposed to be a partnership, and it's pretty well formed before the actual wedding ever takes place. From the way Brian acted after the volleyball game and the way he's ignoring your concerns about the house, I'd say this is a poor example of a partnership."

Melissa fumed, angry once again because his words so closely reflected her own feelings. "And just when did you become such an expert on relationships?"

"I'm not an expert. But it doesn't take an expert to see that Beverly Marshall has her son on a leash and plans to put you on one, too. Brian's so busy playing glory boy he doesn't even notice."

She had no answer for him. What could she say? He was right and they both knew it. Clenching her fists at her side, she stood up and walked to his drafting table.

The exterior drawing of her future home lay in the middle of it. She ran her finger across the smooth paper. It was going to be a beautiful house, but it was becoming harder and harder to picture herself and Brian living there together. Looking up, she watched the rain pounding against the window.

She hadn't heard Morgan move, but he was there behind her, turning her to face him, tipping her chin up until she had no choice but to look him in the eyes. "Damn it, woman! You deserve to be treated better than that!" His eyes flashed down at her. It wasn't until she heard the thunder outside that she realized what she'd seen was the reflection of lightning in his eyes.

Startled, she reached out to him. As her alarm faded, she noticed that her hands were lying on Morgan's chest. Luckily, they'd landed on area covered by his shirt, but she could still tell her initial impression of hardness had been right.

"Um . . . sorry about that." Her fingers moved

gently against the flesh-warmed fabric of his shirt, longing to journey over into the uncovered area. "I'm not a big fan of electrical storms." She reluctantly pulled her hands away.

"I never used to be," Morgan chuckled.

Melissa backed away from him slowly. Part of her wished he'd reach out and pull her into his arms and hold her tightly against the solid wall of his chest.

She turned to the window just in time to see the next bolt of lightning flash across the sky. Knowing the thunder was coming kept her reaction to a minimum. She walked back to the couch and picked up her purse. "Thanks for your time, Morgan."

"You're not going to leave now, are you?"

"I've asked what I came to ask." *And got more than I wanted to hear in return.*

"If I remember correctly, electrical storms here are usually short-lived. Why don't we rustle something up in the kitchen and wait it out."

"Kitchen?"

He opened the second door. "Kitchen."

"Shower, kitchen . . . all the comforts of home." She smiled.

"Not quite *all*—" He quirked one eyebrow up as he looked at her before turning and entering the kitchen.

Could he be referring to a bedroom? Why? Was he flirting with her? Impossible! She'd been right there in front of him, her hands on his chest. He could have put his arms around her, he could have kissed her, but he'd showed no sign of doing either—

just an amused reference to changing his views on electrical storms.

The next flash of lightning broke her concentration and sent her after Morgan into the kitchen.

"Need any help?" she asked.

"No. I'm almost finished. I knew I was going to be working late tonight, so I ordered extra sandwiches from the deli at lunchtime."

During their meal, the storm continued, but they didn't notice. They talked about books, movies, childhood memories, places they'd been and places they'd like to go to. No mention was made of Brian or Beverly.

Instead of fizzling out while they ate, the storm strengthened. Melissa looked at her watch. "This isn't as short-lived as I thought it would be. I'm sorry I disrupted your work schedule."

"Don't worry about it. That's one of the perks of working for yourself . . . a flexible schedule."

"But you *do* have deadlines."

"And I haven't missed one yet."

With the next flash of lightning the lights flickered. Melissa jumped.

"Don't worry. Even if the main power goes out, the building has its own generators."

Ten minutes later the lights flickered again and then went out. There were a few feeble flashes, but after that the lights stayed off.

Morgan swore under his breath.

"The generators?" Melissa asked.

"They don't appear to be working. The lights

would be back on by now. There's a flashlight in my desk. I'll be right back.''

Melissa walked over toward the window. As long as she walked in a straight line, she knew the way was free of obstacles. She reached the window safely and looked down. The headlights of the cars on the street below and a few twinkling lights in the direction of the water were the only breaks in the total darkness.

A light flicked on in Morgan's office. He must have found the flashlight. The light was dim, but it was better than nothing.

''I need to get new batteries for this thing,'' Morgan said once he was back in the workroom. He went into the kitchen and came back with a portable radio. ''Let's see if we can find out anything about this power outage.''

They both sat down on the couch with the radio between them. They found that the outage affected several pockets of the city—one of them being the downtown area. The biggest problem was the severe traffic tangles caused by the lack of traffic lights. Everyone was asked to stay put if at all possible.

''Won't be the first time I've slept at the office,'' Morgan remarked.

''Aren't you forgetting something?''

''What's that?''

''Me!''

''You'll have to stay, too.''

''I can't stay here with you.''

''It's not safe for you to leave.''

''I don't think Brian would like the idea.''

"That has nothing to do with it. Come on, Melly. We're either going to find a way to share the couch or one of us will end up on the floor. It's not like we're spending the night together comfortably in a bed."

Comfortable was not the first word that came to mind when she thought of being in a bed with Morgan. Melissa felt the blood rushing to her cheeks. She was glad for the dim light that kept Morgan from noticing her blush. "But still . . ."

"Listen . . . let's say for the sake of argument that Brian was at an interview with a female reporter and they found themselves in a similar situation. You'd expect him to do the safe thing and stay put, wouldn't you?"

"Well . . . I suppose so."

Morgan laughed.

"What's so funny?"

"I was just thinking. What if the reporter turned out to be the mystery fan who flashed her tattoos to the camera at the World Series."

Melissa wasn't amused by Morgan's thought any more than she had been amused at the game when a masked woman had thrown open her blouse to reveal her Mighty Marshall tattoos.

"What? No come back?" Morgan shone the flashlight in her direction.

"What's to say? Brian's got lots of fans. Many of them are women."

"Think you can cope with it on a regular basis? Aren't you worried that he's bedding down with some fan even as we speak?" He adjusted himself more comfortably on the couch. "Is that why you're afraid to confront him on the issue of his mother's interference . . . afraid he'll run off and sleep with one of his groupies to punish you?"

"How dare you imply . . ." Her back stiffened in anger. "Oh, I get it . . . you're judging Brian by your standards."

"Guess again, angel." His smile gleamed in the dim light. "Last time I looked, architects didn't have groupies."

"You're jealous."

"I'm what?"

"Jealous of Brian."

"Jealous of an immature glory boy who's so full of his own image and his mommy that he can't see what a . . ." The flashlight started to flicker. "Damn. We'd better turn this off for now and save it for an emergency."

"All right, and I think we should turn off the topic of conversation, too. But before we do, let me say that I trust Brian completely."

It was almost a relief not to have to look at Morgan's chest beneath his still-unbuttoned shirt. But hearing his voice in the dark was almost as unnerving. It seemed deeper, smoother, more intimate—flowing over her in darkness broken only by the occasional flash of lightning.

"I hope he earns that trust better than he earned your trust in his ability to keep his mother from meddling with the house plans."

"I thought we were going to change the subject?"

"We were. Which side of the couch do you want to sleep on?"

"Maybe we could just sit here and talk." The thought of lying down next to Morgan, even in opposite directions, was more than she was prepared to handle.

"You want to talk *all* night?"

"Just until the electricity comes back on and it's safe to leave."

"That might be all night . . ."

Morgan took a deep breath. His housekeeping service must have changed detergents. He liked this new one. It smelled soft—almost but not quite floral. Nuzzling in closer, he sniffed again. The pillow case even felt different—smooth, silky.

His eyes came open slowly. He hadn't gotten enough sleep, and his mind was fuzzy. Nevertheless, he immediately recognized the honey-blond hair he was nuzzling, but it took him a while to realize he and Melissa were lying on the couch in his office and remember why they were there.

What was the last thing he remembered? Oh, yes, knock-knock and elephant jokes. It had been late, they'd both gotten fed up with fighting, neither one could sleep even after they'd changed out of their uncomfortable professional clothes and into two of the sweatsuits he kept on hand to wear after hours, so they'd started telling old jokes. But when had they stopped talking, and how on earth had she ended up in his arms?

Not that he minded. She felt terrific! He tucked

his arms more tightly around her, running his hands up and down her back.

Oh, God, she wasn't wearing anything underneath the sweatshirt. He was suddenly aware of the softness of her breasts against his chest and then the rest of her pressed close to him, their legs tangled.

He bit back the groan that threatened to escape him. No doubt about it, it was time to get moving on his social life again. The first month or so when he set up shop in a city was always hectic and left little time for socializing.

The heat raging through his body told him he was way overdue for some socializing. He tried to picture what the next lady in his life would look like, but all he kept seeing was Melly.

Damn! He should have never let her in last night.

He had been glad to learn that she wasn't living with Marshall. Were they sleeping together? He hated the idea of Marshall touching her, let alone kissing or making love to her. *Not much you can do about that, buddy,* he thought grimly. *She's engaged to the guy.*

Last night she had accused him of being jealous of Marshall. In general he wasn't, but he did envy the other man his woman. Especially since the moron didn't even appreciate what a treasure he had.

Melissa crawled slowly out of sleep. She'd been dreaming about Morgan—an old dream, a familiar dream—the wedding dream. It had been so real. It seemed like she could still feel the hard wall of his chest against her cheek and his arms wrapped around her.

She yawned, then opened her eyes slowly. Well . . . she thought she'd opened her eyes, but the gray sweatshirt stretched across firm male muscles told her otherwise. Somehow the Morgan in her dreams had acquired clothes and after she'd so carefully removed his others . . . she'd just have to start over.

She began to slide over so she could grab the bottom of the sweatshirt, but started to fall until the hard arms around her pulled her back, saving her from hitting the floor and pulling her out of the last remnants of sleep into total wakefulness.

She looked behind her and saw the edge of a couch, not a bed. Looking back to the front her eyes locked with Morgan's.

"Good morning, Melly."

"Good morning," she managed to say, despite her discomfort at being pressed against him. She'd lain like this with him countless times in her dreams, but the reality of it was so much more than she'd imagined.

"You can use my phone if you'd like to call Brian."

"Brian?"

"Brian." He reached down and held her left hand in front of her.

The large diamond solitaire winked in the morning light.

Brian . . . how could she have forgotten?

FOUR

"Brian's in San Francisco."

"My phone can handle long-distance calls. I make them all the time." His voice had a morning huskiness to it.

She could feel his words rumble through his chest, as well as every breath he took. His hands were making lazy patterns across her back—her nerve endings still feeling his touch even after his hands moved on to weave their magic elsewhere. She shifted restlessly against him, but it only made things worse.

Her breasts felt swollen and heavy, her nipples hard and tight. Tension raced through the muscles of her stomach where she lay against his hip—and when it came to legs, she wasn't sure where each of them began and ended.

With a frustrated cry, Melissa jumped out of his embrace and off the couch. She ran damp hands nervously down her thighs.

Morgan stayed on the couch, stretched out over most of its length. He rose halfway, resting his weight on his elbows, and watched her.

"Listen, thanks for letting me stay, because of the storm and all." She quickly began gathering up her things. "And I'm really sorry you didn't get any work done. I'll wash the sweatsuit and get it back to you. Thanks for letting me borrow it."

She knew she was babbling, but couldn't seem to slow down. Her heart was racing, and she could feel the blood pulsing through her veins. She began backing out of the room.

"You don't have to rush off. How about breakfast? There's a restaurant downstairs, I'll call and have them send something up."

"Oh, no, thank you. The rain's stopped, the lights are on, so I'm sure the street lights are working—and I've taken up enough of your time already." She needed to get out of here before she gave in to the impulse to get right back on the couch with all that gorgeous masculinity.

Morgan stood up and followed her. "I'm going to have breakfast anyway. You're more than welcome to join me."

"I've got to go." Her voice sounded desperate to her own ears.

"Another time, maybe?"

"Maybe."

She couldn't get out of there fast enough. It wasn't until she stepped out of the carpeted building and onto the cold concrete of the parking garage that she realized all she had on her feet were the socks Morgan had loaned her.

Walking carefully on tiptoe she reached her car and headed for home. There were still puddles and a few palm fronds scattered about, but all other signs of last night's weather were gone. The sky was a clear rain-washed blue and the sun shone brightly.

How had she ended up in his arms? Had she thrown herself at him, had they kissed? She hoped not, because if she ever got to kiss Morgan, she wanted to remember every sweet second of it.

What on earth was she thinking? She shouldn't be thinking about kissing Morgan. But drat, how she wished she could remember what had happened last night. It really bothered her. And what must Morgan be thinking?

Since she was moving in the opposite direction from most of the morning traffic, the ride home was smooth and easy.

"Where did you get stranded?" Carol asked as Melissa walked into the apartment. "I got stuck at my mother's, of all places! She woke me up at five o'clock to feed me a seven-course breakfast. She sent some muffins home with me. You hungry?"

"Yes, actually I am." She set her clothes from yesterday and her purse on the couch.

They went into the kitchen and Carol gave Melissa a muffin and cup of coffee. Melissa walked over and sat at the dining-room table.

"So . . . where were you?"

Melissa bit into the muffin. "This is wonderful. Pumpkin?"

"And persimmon."

"They're very good."

"Lissa . . ." Carol sounded exasperated. "I promise to get you the recipe if you'll just answer my question!"

"I was stuck downtown at Morgan's office."

"Morgan Edwards, of the glorious blue eyes and oh-so-magnificent buns?"

"Do I know any other Morgans?"

"I don't know. Do you?"

"No."

Carol gave a long, slow whistle. "And?" she prompted.

Melissa gave Carol a brief rundown on why she'd gone to Morgan's office and the events which had followed.

"I can't believe the nerve of that woman."

"Me, either." Melissa took a sip of her coffee. "That situation on its own would be bad enough, but on top of it all, there's Morgan."

"It's hard to imagine him waking up with you in his arms and not trying to kiss you. Almost seems like it would be a natural reflex of sorts."

"I should be grateful for his exceptional willpower."

"But you're not," Carol stated.

"I want very much to say 'Of course I am.' " She leaned her elbow on the table and rested her forehead on her hand. "But if I'm really honest with myself, I have to admit that I'm disappointed and feeling a bit slighted."

"I'd probably feel the same way. I'll bet he's a terrific kisser."

Melissa straightened up in her chair and looked at Carol. "Probably, but it's obvious that all the electricity I feel when I'm around him is completely one-sided."

"Or he may just be an absolute gentleman about not moving in on someone else's territory."

"Doesn't sound very plausible."

"But you have to admit, it's a possibility."

"Anything's possible." Melissa shrugged her shoulders.

"So what are you going to do?"

"When Brian gets back from San Francisco, I'm going to talk to him about his mother's interfering. If he doesn't agree to do something about it, then I'll have to decide whether or not to cancel the wedding."

"And Morgan?"

"I'm hoping time will lessen my reaction to him."

"But what if he *is* interested in you?"

"He's given no sign of it, so I'm assuming he's not." She tapped her fingers on the side of her mug. "I made the decision to marry Brian before Morgan or Beverly arrived on the scene. Without the two of them here, I was in a much more stable frame of mind. I fell in love, accepted Brian's proposal, and never doubted my choices. Now, until I get my emotions back under control, I'm going to trust in the plans I made before all this chaos hit."

Friday morning, Morgan headed out to the Marshall lot. Mr. Stevens had called and they were going to start leveling and grading procedures. He had a basic outline and measurements of the outer perimeters of the house, but he hadn't done up a final blueprint. He needed to talk with Brian and Melissa to see if the original floor plan was still a go, or if they wanted Beverly's changes implemented.

He almost dreaded the thought of talking to Melly. He was still haunted by her scent and the feel of her snuggled up against him.

When she first awakened and smiled at him, he thought maybe she felt the same attraction for him that he felt for her. Then he had to spoil the mood by mentioning Brian. It had just popped out, as though part of him was trying to remind him she was spoken for and he shouldn't be feeling anything for her.

Once he mentioned Brian, she seemed to withdraw from him completely. She'd rushed out of there in no time, refusing his offer for breakfast.

He was a fool not to have just leaned over and kissed her. No, that wouldn't have been such a good idea.

A knot formed in the pit of his stomach as he remembered the last time he'd kissed a woman with someone else's engagement ring on her finger.

He'd been out of school for a few years and was working for an architectural firm in Atlanta. His reputation in the field was developing rapidly. Several impressed clients had offered him financing if he wanted to open his own firm.

He met Emmie Rhodes at a party. Her father was one of the firm's clients, and Morgan had been one of the principal designers of his new bank building.

Her fiancé, Robert Borland, was high up in the ranks of Mr. Rhodes's bank.

Although attracted to her, he would have stayed miles away if Emmie hadn't come on to him. He fell in love with her. He fell hard.

When Robert called off the wedding, Emmie turned to Morgan. They moved in together and began making wedding plans of their own. Things were going well, but then the ex-fiancé had started coming around. With Morgan's moral support, Emmie had sent him on his way. . . .

Until one day, Robert must have come up with the right offer or displayed the proper amount of misery and contrition. Emmie came to Morgan's office, returned his ring, and thanked him for his part in helping Robert see the light. All her personal belongings were out of the apartment when he got home that evening.

He'd felt like someone had ripped his heart from his body. Never again, he'd promised himself, never again. Since then there had been plenty of other women—some just friends, some friends and lovers, but none had touched his heart.

But now there was Melly. . . .

He reached the lot and went into the portable trailer Mr. Stevens had set up for use during the construction. They worked together, going over the plan and materials lists.

Around noon, there was a knock at the door.

"Come in," Mr. Stevens hollered.

Morgan was surprised to see Brian. Alerted, he

braced himself for the sight of Melly, but Brian simply closed the door and walked toward them.

Greetings were exchanged. Morgan feigned civility, reminding himself that Brian was a client. Brian sat down at the table. There was another knock at the door. This time it was one of the workers, needing Mr. Stevens.

"Will you two excuse me for a minute? This shouldn't take long."

"No problem," Morgan answered.

"Guess everything's running smoothly," Brian remarked.

"I'm at a standstill at the moment. Your mother has contacted me about making several changes in the floor plan."

Brian waved his hand in the air. "Whatever . . ."

One eyebrow rose in astonishment. "Aren't you going to ask what the changes are?"

"I trust Mother's judgment."

"What about Melly's feelings on this?"

"I'm sure it doesn't matter one way or another to *Lissa*."

Melly must not have confronted him yet. He wondered what she was waiting for. Had she changed her mind? Was she going to let herself be dominated after all? "I think you'd better check with her first. You might find she cares a great deal."

Brian frowned. "I think I'm in a better position to know what Lissa does or does not care about than you are."

Morgan laughed. He couldn't believe this guy. "And if I told you that I know otherwise for a fact?"

"Lissa's talked to Luc about this and he's passed word on to you?"

Morgan shrugged noncommittally. Obviously Melly hadn't told Brian about going to see him in his office and spending the night. Oh, how he would love to tell him about waking up with Melly in his arms and how for just a moment she hadn't even remembered who Brian was.

If looks could kill, the one Brian shot him would have done the trick in record time. "I'll discuss it with her and get back to you on Monday. Is that early enough for you?"

"Monday will be fine."

"Good." Brian's reply was crisp and tight. He left the trailer, slamming the door behind him.

Morgan went over to the window and watched Brian talking with the workmen, shaking hands . . . the whole P.R. routine.

He wished he could see Brian's reaction when Melly told him she did want a say in the plans for the house.

How the Mighty Marshall will fall!

Melissa hadn't gotten the chance to talk to Brian on Thursday. His plane was delayed and it was eleven o'clock at night before he got back to his house. They set a dinner date for Friday evening.

On Friday's lunch hour, she had arranged to pick Carol up at the preschool where she worked and take her along for the first fitting of her wedding gown.

Melissa held her breath as she and Carol waited for the saleslady to return with her dress.

"This is it, kiddo," Carol said.

"I know."

"Still feeling unsure?"

"Yes."

Carol patted her arm. "You'll feel better after you've talked with Brian tonight."

"I hope you're right."

The woman returned from the back of the store and their conversation stopped.

"That's not my dress," Melissa told her.

She checked the tag. "Melissa Ellison?" She showed the tag to Melissa.

"Yes, that's me. But this is not my dress. I ordered ivory satin, not white."

The woman hung the dress on a display hook and went over to the order book on her desk. She found the page she was looking for. "Ah, I remember now. You *had* ordered the ivory satin, but Mrs. Marshall called on your behalf the next day and changed the order to white."

Melissa went and looked in the book. "I see." She bit her tongue to hold back her anger. After all, it wasn't this woman's fault. "The problem is that I never authorized Mrs. Marshall to call you."

"Oh, my dear, I am so sorry. She had been with you the day you picked out the dress and when she called I just assumed . . ." She was genuinely distressed. "I will put in a rush reorder immediately and we should have the right dress in by next week. That will still give us more than enough time to make any necessary alterations." She started to reach for her pen.

"No." Melissa glanced at Carol, then back to the saleslady. "I'd like to think about it first. I'll call you when I've made up my mind."

"All right. You have my card?"

"Yes, I still have it. Thank you."

Melissa and Carol left the store. "Lissa, are you thinking about keeping the white dress?"

"No."

"Then why didn't you let her order the ivory dress today?"

"There may not be a wedding."

Melissa dropped Carol off at work and went over to Brian's. He wasn't there, but Beverly said he was going to stop by the lot on his way to a team photo session.

It took every ounce of willpower she had to keep from confronting Beverly face-to-face. But she refused to play control games with the other woman for Brian's support. He would either be one hundred percent behind her in making Beverly see her place or the marriage was off.

"Oh, that's just what I need," she bit out as she pulled into the lot and saw the red Ferrari. Luckily, she saw no sign of Morgan in the immediate vicinity.

She spotted Brian standing a few feet away, talking to a workman. She got out of her car and went over to them.

After Brian greeted her and introduced her to the project foreman, she asked if she could have a word with him alone. They started walking slowly to the back of the lot.

"I went in for the initial fitting of my wedding gown today," she began.

"Great! Things are really moving along." He reached down and took her hand.

"It was the wrong dress."

"The wrong dress?"

"Yes. Apparently your mother called the store and changed the dress from ivory to white."

"Honey, you're entitled to wear white."

He didn't seem to understand what all the fuss was about. "Brian, what I'm entitled to has nothing to do with this! I'd chosen to wear ivory. That's my decision and *only* my decision to make. It's none of your mother's business."

"There is still enough time before the wedding, can't they get the right dress in?"

"As a matter of fact, they can." She put her hand on his arm to stop him. They were now far enough away from any of the workmen that they wouldn't be overheard. "But that's like putting a Band-Aid on a broken bone. Something has got to be done about your mother's interfering."

Brian looked down at her. He ran his hand softly down her cheek. "I'll tell her to leave the wedding plans to you." He started to lean forward to kiss her.

Melissa put her hands on his chest and held him back. "She's also been calling Morgan about the house."

Brian shook his head. "So I've heard." There was an angry edge to his voice.

Melissa assumed Morgan had talked to Brian. She

wondered what had been said. "I don't want any changes made without our mutual approval."

Brian looked surprised. "I didn't think it mattered one way or another."

"I *did* mention it in the car on Tuesday."

"Sorry, Lissa. I had a lot on my mind that day. Guess I wasn't listening very well."

"Guess you weren't."

"I'll take care of it." He still didn't sound like he cared much.

"Brian, this is going to be our house. We're the ones who are going to have to live in it day in and day out. We need to be happy with it."

"I don't see what the big deal is, as long as there are four walls and a roof."

"It's important to me."

"All right. I said I'd take care of it and I will."

"Will that be the end of it? What about the rest of our lives? Is she going to have her hands in that, too?"

"Honey, she means well . . ."

"But she's running roughshod over every decision we make."

"She wants to help."

"There's help, Brian, and then there's manipulation."

"She's my mother. I can't just shut her out."

"I don't want her shut out of your—our lives. She can make all the suggestions, or even criticisms, she wants. But I refuse to let her make our decisions for us or change decisions we've already made."

"It's not going to be easy." He sighed. "She started this after my father died. During the years he was bedridden, she got used to having total responsibility for the two of them. Once he died, she switched all her time and concern to me and I didn't have the heart to tell her to stop. I wanted to make things easy for her.''

"Making things easier for her doesn't mean you let her walk all over you. There's a big difference between the two. Besides, if she wasn't so busy running *your* life, she might be able to start a new life of her own."

Brian's watch alarm beeped. He pulled Melissa into his arms and kissed her briefly. When she offered very little response, he frowned. "I've got to go. Let's cancel tonight's dinner. I'll talk to Mother instead and pick you up in the morning and take you to breakfast."

"All right."

Brian walked her back to her car and opened the door for her to get in, closing it once she was seated. "I'll see you in the morning, Lissa." Without waiting for her to respond, he turned away.

She watched Brian walk to his car, get in, and drive away. What had happened to the dream of building their first home? His mother had turned it into a quest for higher resale value. And where was the love, the joy, the celebration?

Melissa's concentration was broken by the overpoweringly masculine body blocking her view. One arm resting on the top of her car, Morgan leaned down to look in at her.

"Trouble in paradise?"

FIVE

The teasing smile faded from Morgan's face. "Melly, are you all right?"

Melissa looked up at him. "Am I all right?" She shrugged. "I have no idea." She started to put her keys in the ignition, but Morgan reached through the window and stopped her.

"Come on. You could use some cheering up." He opened her door, helped her out, grabbed her purse from the passenger seat, rolled up the window and locked her car.

They were in his car and moving before she knew it. "Morgan, where are we going?"

"From my vast wealth of experience," he told her in a professorial tone, "I have learned that the best cure for your ailment is a hot-fudge sundae."

"McCoy's?" She smiled at him.

"Unless you'd rather go somewhere else."

"No, McCoy's is fine." She sat back more comfortably into the soft leather of the bucket seat. "Nice car."

"Thanks. I like it."

"A big change from your Bug."

"Ah, yes and no."

"I can see the yes, but why no?"

"Because as I was buzzing around town in my VW, I used to pretend I was driving a Ferrari."

Melissa laughed. "Planning ahead?"

"Big dreams." He smiled over at her. "You laughed. My cure is working already."

McCoy's Ice Cream Parlor had redecorated and added frozen yogurt to their menu since they'd been there last, but they still served the old standard hot-fudge sundae with whipped cream, chopped nuts, and a cherry on top.

"Feeling better?" Morgan asked as her spoon hit the whipped cream.

"Yes. This was a great idea. Thanks, Morgan."

"Anytime," he assured her. "Do you feel like talking about it?"

"Not right now." She wasn't sure she was ready for any of Morgan's cut-right-to-the-heart-of-the-matter speeches.

"All right. But can I ask one question?"

"One."

"Did you finally lay down the law about his mother?"

"Yes."

"He didn't look very happy when he left."

"No, I don't suppose he was." She reached across the table, picked up Morgan's spoon, and handed it to him. "I thought we weren't going to talk about this."

"Right." He dug into his sundae.

"What were you doing at the site, Morgan?"

"Going over the materials list with Stevens—and I usually try to be on hand the first day of construction on my projects."

"Why?"

"To me architecture is an art. Sculptors touch the marble that will become their statues, painters wallow in their paint, and I need to feel close to the site and materials of my buildings to truly feel the art of their creation."

Melissa could see the excitement for his work shining in his eyes and sense the artistic energy flowing out of him as he talked about his work. "I've never looked at houses or buildings quite that way before."

"Most people haven't."

"Which do you like best. The commercial buildings or the houses?"

"I enjoy both. The commercial buildings are awe-inspiring in many cases because of their size. But the houses are special because they give me a chance to blend my work in with nature. So much of the time with commercial structures, I'm designing or redesigning in the proverbial concrete jungle. I'd like to do a large corporate project on a rural lot or resort designing one of these days."

"Why don't you?"

"I've been trying, but I haven't won any contracts of that nature yet. I've got several bids out at the moment."

"Good luck with them." She set her spoon down next to her empty sundae glass. "It must be nice to love what you do for a living."

"Don't you like your job?"

"I enjoy the work and it's gratifying to see the business growing and succeeding. But the business was there and on solid footing when I started. It's not the same as starting something of my own from scratch and making a go of it."

"Why don't you start your own business?"

"I've thought about it, but I don't want to let the family down."

"You could start your own advertising, marketing, or public relations firm and keep the sporting goods stores as a client."

"I like the idea." She wouldn't be leaving the family out in the cold, but she could expand her own horizons and create and strive for her own goals.

Long after their sundaes were gone, they continued to talk. Despite the turmoil of the last few weeks, Melissa realized she felt happy and at peace. She knew her newfound tranquility was probably short-lived, but that didn't stop her enjoyment of it now.

"Well, I guess I'd better get you back to your car."

Melissa looked down at her watch. Where had the time gone? Morgan paid the check and they left.

They drove back to the lot in silence, Melissa's

mind reliving their last drive home from a sundae outing.

Morgan pulled up next to her car, now alone on the lot, and shut off the car's ignition. Once the powerful purring of the engine faded away, they were surrounded by silence. The late-afternoon shadows stretched across the leveled ground, disproportionately long when compared to the trees they came from.

Melissa was reluctant to leave the comfortable confines of Morgan's car. She had had a wonderful afternoon and didn't want it to end.

"Thank you for cheering me up," she said, smiling at him.

"Like I said earlier . . . anytime." He reached out, took her hand, and gave it a squeeze. "If you decide later on that you want to talk, give me a call."

"I appreciate that." The hard warmth of his hand surrounded hers, sending sparks of awareness racing through her. Now more than ever, she didn't want to leave. Her eyes locked with his. Was he feeling the same way she was?

"Do you love Brian, Melly?"

His question stunned her. Not just because he asked it, but because she was suddenly unsure of the answer. "I thought I did. In high school and college, I didn't do much more than casual dating. I was pretty busy with my studies and working at the stores. I'd go out with someone a few times and that would be the end of it . . ." Once they realized she wasn't going to help them earn another notch on their bedpost!

"It was different with Marshall?"

"Brian kept coming back. He made me feel very special. I thought that special feeling was love. But I don't know . . . lately I've been so confused . . .'' Especially when Morgan was around. She could feel tears of frustration welling up in her eyes. She blinked rapidly to hold them back, but one escaped to run down her cheek.

"Hey, no tears." Morgan's voice washed over her, pushing her mind back to another time when he'd said the same thing.

Appearing to move in slow motion, his hand came up to brush the tear away. Her heart skipped a beat as he kissed her cheek.

She turned toward him, her hands clasping his upper arms. Looking deeply into his eyes, she saw a puzzled flicker before they flashed with desire. His gaze dropped to her lips.

"Kiss me . . . please." She hadn't planned to say it, but once the words were out, she knew it was what she wanted. "You promised," she reminded him.

She tightened her grip on his arms to prevent his pulling away. Her efforts were not needed. When he moved, he moved toward her, closing the space between them.

His lips were hard and warm against hers, aggressively coaxing her into full response. She had waited ten years for his kiss and every minute had been worth it. None of her fantasies had even come close.

The memories of all the kisses she'd shared in her life paled as she parted her lips to give him more intimate access.

The tingling sensations flowed through her body . . . much stronger than what she'd been feeling just by being around him. She moved her arms up around his neck. His slid down the length of her back to pull her as close to him as possible with the car's seating arrangements.

The kiss seemed to go on forever, but still she didn't want it to end. For a long time, it was enough. But then she found herself being tormented by various parts of her body.

Her hands, running through the ends of the hair on his neck, longed to move to the front, unbutton his shirt and fully explore as they'd wanted to do on Tuesday evening. Her breasts, swollen and pressed against his chest, ached to be touched. The lower parts of her body sent phantom messages of being aligned with Morgan's male counterparts. Her toes were curled so tightly she thought her shoes might burst.

What shocked her the most was the intensity of the desires building up within her. She had never experienced anything of this magnitude before.

Morgan was the first to pull back, but he did it slowly, leaving several short, soft kisses on her still-parted lips before moving completely away.

Melissa's eyes fluttered open and locked with his for a long moment as her mind ran through an instant replay. If he asked her to go home with him, she knew she would. If he wanted to make love to her, she knew she would let him. At this moment she knew she would deny this man nothing.

But he didn't ask for anything. . . .

He ran his hand down her cheek once more before escorting her back to her car.

"If you need to talk, call me."

"All right."

A gentle squeeze of her shoulder and he was gone, back to his car.

He followed her for as long as their paths home were the same, then flashed his lights at her before turning right as she continued on.

Melissa took a deep breath and slowly released it. That had been quite a kiss. It had been nothing like kissing Brian.

She wished now that Morgan had kissed her on Tuesday night or Wednesday morning. It would have saved her a lot of time, soul-searching and trying to make a decision.

Knowing the effect Morgan's kiss had on her, there was no way she could marry Brian!

Morgan couldn't sleep. It was only four o'clock in the morning, but he was wide-awake. He couldn't seem to get Melly out of his mind.

He could still feel her in his arms, feel her lips pressed against his in a kiss that had rocked through him all the way down to his toes. He had never been so deeply moved by just a kiss before.

God—what would happen if he made love to her?

This afternoon, he had wanted to restart his car and bring her back here. Would she have come?

What wouldn't he give to have her lying beside him right now—curled up against his side—love-tousled, sleek, and satisfied.

Suddenly too warm, he threw off his blankets, then shivered as the cool night air hit his overheated body.

There was no way he could just sit back and let Melly marry Marshall. He'd have to go to her and lay it on the line. Ask her to call off or postpone the wedding, give him a chance to prove she belonged with him instead.

He might not make as much money as Marshall, and while he was starting to be well known in his field he didn't have the star status a baseball player had. But he didn't think it would matter to Melly. He certainly had much more to offer her in the areas of respect and consideration for her feelings.

"You're getting rather cocky, pal, thinking you can walk off with the fiancée of the Professional Athlete of the Year. She might just laugh in your face." He plumped up his pillow, then settled back, his hands beneath his head. "But she didn't laugh when I kissed her." He would go see her in the morning and talk to her about it.

Yes, that's exactly what he would do.

"Ready to go?" Brian asked.

"Maybe we should talk here," Melissa suggested. "It's more private." The least she could do was spare him an audience when she broke off their engagement.

"Carol?"

"She's gone up to L.A. for her nephew's birthday party."

"All right then." Brian came in and sat down on the couch.

"Would you like some coffee? I've already made it."

"No, thanks." He patted the seat beside him. "Why don't you just sit down and we'll talk?"

Melissa sat next to him. He took her hands in his, looking down at them.

"Brian . . ."

"Melissa . . ."

They both spoke at once.

"Go ahead," Melissa offered.

"I've thought a lot about what you said yesterday afternoon."

"Did you talk to your mother about it last night?"

"No."

"No! Brian . . ." Now more than ever she was sure that her decision to call off the engagement was a good one.

"There was no need to." He took a deep breath. "You were right about my letting Mother manipulate me. And I agree that it's time for it to stop." He squeezed her hands tightly. "Before I met you, my agent had been hounding me about settling down and establishing a family to widen my endorsement potential. Then Mother saw the picture in *Sports Illustrated* that was taken at the autograph day in your store and asked if I knew the pretty blonde standing behind me. In retrospect, I should have said no and saved us all this."

"What happened when you told her you knew me?"

"She suggested that I ask you out."

"And you did."

"I had been thinking about it anyway."

"Brian, you don't have to lie to protect my feelings."

"I'm not lying. I *had* thought about it, but you seemed a bit cool and distant. I didn't think you'd be interested."

"So much for my businesslike manners." Melissa gave a hard laugh.

"Your business manners were perfect, very professional. What I meant was that your only interest in me seemed to be on that level. There were none of the subtle body-language come-ons or long smoldering looks I get from a lot of the women I meet on a professional basis. After we'd had a few dates, Mom started hinting that you'd be a good wife for me. That and my agent's prompting are what made me decide it was time for me to get married."

"So you proposed?"

"Yes." He nodded. "But last night I realized . . . Damn, honey, this is hard for me to say." He took her in his arms, resting his chin on the top of her head. "I can't marry you."

Melissa didn't say a word. She thought about telling him she'd been going to call off the wedding anyway, but decided against it. He had finally made his own decision on something and she didn't want to devalue this first independent move on his part.

"Lissa, please understand there's nothing against

you personally in this. You are a beautiful, intelligent, desirable woman . . . I'm just not ready for marriage.''

She pulled back to look up at him. "It's okay, Brian. I do understand." She reached down and took off the engagement ring.

"You're a very special woman, and if I were ready for marriage, you'd be the one." He took the ring from her and put it in his pocket. "You sure you're all right?"

"Yes, I'm fine."

"Guess I'd better be going then."

Melissa stood up, walked over to the front door and opened it for him. "Good-bye, Brian."

He leaned down and kissed her on the forehead. " 'Bye, Lissa."

Half an hour later there was another knock at the door. She wondered who it could be. Brian couldn't have changed his mind.

"Morgan, good morning." Snug blue jeans and form-hugging sweatshirt—the man should come with a surgeon general's warning label.

"Hope it's not too early."

"Not at all. Come in." She stepped back to let him into the apartment.

Once in, Morgan picked up her left hand and looked at her ring finger. "You broke your engagement?" He smiled at her.

"Actually, I planned to, but Brian beat me to it." Melissa expected to be swept up in his arms, but he didn't move.

"Marshall broke it off?" His smile faded.

"Only because I let him talk first."

He let go of her hand and backed up a step. "Well, I think in time you'll realize it was for the best."

"I realize it now. I'd already made up my mind to call off the wedding yesterday afternoon." Why was he acting so strange—so cold? She had expected him to be happy the wedding was off. She'd expected him to want to pick up where they'd left off in his car.

"Yesterday afternoon?"

"Late afternoon . . . early evening."

"After—" he stopped.

"After you kissed me, Morgan."

For a moment she thought she saw a flash of pleasure in his eyes, then he shuttered his emotions from her. "You were going to cancel your engagement because I kissed you?"

The way he said it made it sound like a crazy harebrained scheme.

"Yes."

"Feeling guilty?"

"No." How could she explain to him the strong effect his kiss had had on her when he seemed so unmoved by it.

"Not guilt, then what?"

"I thought maybe you and I . . ." If there had been any of the desire she'd seen in his eyes yesterday, she would have been able to finish her sentence. But he was looking at her like he had after the Valentine episode—patiently indulgent.

He rested his hands on her shoulders. "It was just a kiss between two consenting adults. Don't try to make it into anything else, Melissa."

"I see." Melissa looked down. She didn't want him to see the disappointment she felt. She refused to give him the satisfaction. Obviously the kiss hadn't affected him the way it had affected her.

It had felt so different, so wonderful. But maybe it was run of the mill to him. Maybe her imagination had been playing tricks on her. Knowing she'd expected kissing him to be special, perhaps her mind had obliged by making it seem somehow more than it was.

One thing she knew, there was no way she was going to let him know how much his attitude hurt her. "So, can I get you some coffee, herbal tea?"

"Nothing, thanks. I need to be going." He turned and reached for the doorknob. Looking back over his shoulder, he asked, "Are you going to be all right?"

"Of course." She flashed him a bright, perky smile she was far from feeling.

"Like I said, I think not marrying Marshall is in your best interest." He opened the door, turning once more to look back at her. "Good-bye, Melly."

" 'Bye, Morgan." If he didn't get out of here soon, she was going to throw herself at him and beg him to stay, to give the two of them a chance at a relationship, or at the very least to kiss her again.

Finally he left, closing the door behind him. She hadn't realized she'd been holding her breath until the air forced its way out of her lungs.

When Brian had left she'd felt a sense of relief,

like a weight lifting off her shoulders. She'd felt the same elation a traveler feels as they accelerate back onto the highway after maneuvering through a convoluted detour.

And she'd felt hope. Hope that now she was unattached, Morgan would make his move. Obviously she'd been wrong.

She'd told Carol the other day that the electricity she felt must be one-sided. Guess she'd been right. So much for Carol's theory that Morgan was holding back because she was engaged.

But he'd kissed her? *Sure, after you'd practically begged him to*, she reminded herself.

She walked over to the couch, sat down, curling her legs up underneath her, resting her chin on her knees.

So where did that leave her? Back at square one. She felt a restlessness, beyond her usual reaction to being with Morgan. Maybe she needed a vacation, or maybe she needed to give serious consideration to Morgan's suggestion that she start her own business.

The responsibilities of a new business would certainly keep her busy. She looked down at her bare ring finger. Her hand felt light. She hadn't realized the ring had been so heavy.

Her engagement to Brian was over, but it was Morgan her heart was missing.

Morgan got behind the wheel of his car and headed north. He drove conservatively when there were other cars around, but when he had the road to himself, he ignored the speed limit signs and avoided looking at his speedometer. He didn't need to know how fast he was going—but he needed to feel the surge. Needed it to keep him from running back to Melly.

All his hopes and plans from the night before had come to a screeching halt when Melly had told him that Marshall had broken their engagement. Physically it felt like someone had punched him in the stomach.

He couldn't let history repeat itself. He refused to let Melly use him the way Emmie had. He wouldn't be a decoy to lure Marshall back to her!

He'd have to put up with a little heartache now to avoid a big heartache later . . . or so his brain told him. But his heart insisted there wasn't any pain greater than what he was feeling right now.

SIX

This week's Sunday dinner was a quiet affair. Everyone offered Melissa their sympathy. She accepted the comfort, but didn't tell them her pain was from losing her chance with Morgan rather than from the broken engagement.

Later that evening, back at the apartment, she talked the whole tangled tale through with Carol. Carol couldn't understand Morgan's sudden coolness, either, and encouraged her not to lose hope completely.

The next week was a busy one for Melissa, even with Carol's help, as she canceled all the plans for the wedding: church, reception site, flowers, invitations, limousines . . . the list seemed endless. She worked backward through all her carefully made plans.

Everyone she contacted was shocked and sympathetic. Someone she talked to must have done more than cancel her order, because as she arrived back at the store after lunch on Tuesday, she found a swarm of reporters waiting for her.

Foremost in the crowd was David Andrews, the morning talk-show host who had dubbed her and Brian San Diego's Royal Couple. He'd interviewed them on his program shortly after their engagement and had been doing a weekly Royal Wedding update ever since.

David stuck his microphone in her face. "Lissa, is it true? Is the wedding off?"

A barrage of questions flew at her from every direction as cameras flashed and videocams rolled.

"Listen, I have nothing to say and we're trying to run a business here. So unless you're here to buy sports equipment, I'd appreciate it if you'd please go." She gestured to the parking lot with her left hand.

"The ring's gone!" David shouted. "Get a shot of her hand, Rich."

"Hey, Lissa, did he dump you?" a voice called out from the back.

"Oh, for heaven's sake!" Melissa jammed both hands in her pockets and began to fight her way out of the crowd. When she was halfway through, her task became easier as her father and the other employees joined together and cleared a path for her.

Once she reached the safety of her office, she called Brian and explained the situation.

"Damn, I'm sorry, Lissa. Guess we need to make

an official statement. Let me call my agent. I'll get right back to you.''

While waiting for Brian's call, she went over the proofs of next week's newspaper ads. It was a struggle concentrating and she welcomed the diversion of her father coming in to tell her the reporters had been sent packing. When the phone rang, she picked it up on the first ring.

"Jim's organizing a press conference for five o'clock. I'd like you to be there if you feel up to it. If you don't, I'll understand.''

"I don't mind.''

"You'll get a chance to read over the statement beforehand, to be sure it meets with your approval.''

"Good.''

"It'll be short and to the point. How do you feel about taking questions afterward?''

"Do we have to?''

"Not if you don't want to.''

Now he decides to value her opinion. "I'd rather not.'' Marriage was a personal matter after all. Even though her relationship with Brian had been a media circus at times, they could still end it with some dignity.

"Fine. I'll have Jim arrange for a car to pick you up at four. Will you be at the store or at home?''

"At home, I need to change clothes first.''

"All right. I'll see you there then.''

Just before five that Tuesday evening, Morgan knocked on Luc's door. He was wearing a sweatshirt, gym shorts, court shoes, and had a racquetball racquet tucked under his arm.

"Come on in," Luc said, opening the door. "We'll head over to the court in a minute. I want to catch the local news first."

Morgan followed Luc into the living room. "Any special reason?"

Before Luc had a chance to answer, he saw the reason. There on the television was Melly, fighting her way through a crowd of reporters outside the sporting goods store.

The newscaster narrated. "Melissa Ellison had no comment when confronted this afternoon. But Jim Hall, Brian Marshall's agent, has called a press conference which is scheduled to start any minute now. Live on the scene is David Andrews. David . . ."

"Thanks, Robin." The picture changed to a smiling David. In the background was a microphone-bedecked podium set up on a platform. "Our sources tell us that both Brian and Melissa are here at the hotel, although they arrived separately."

A buzz went up in the room and the camera focused on the podium. Melissa and Brian, followed by an older man, came into view. Morgan wondered where Beverly was.

His heart raced as he looked at Melly's image on the screen. She looked calm, serene, and beautiful as always. Were they reconciling already?

Although he hated to admit it, they made a damn good-looking couple—the blond California health club look. But then again, Melly's fairness was a good contrast for his coloring.

Whoa, boy. He put a halt to the path his mind was wandering in. It didn't matter how well he and Melly looked together. There was no way he was going anywhere near her.

The older man handed Brian a piece of paper. He set it on the podium, then held his hands up to silence the crowd before beginning. "Ladies and gentlemen of the press. There have been a large number of rumors floating around and we'd like to clarify things for you. Ms. Ellison and I *have* canceled our plans for a January wedding." He paused, waiting for the buzz of conversations in the room to die down. "It was an amicable agreement. Marriage is a big step and we realized that we weren't ready."

Questions began immediately, but Brian took Melly's hand and started off the platform, keeping himself between her and the rest of the room.

As the camera followed the retreating couple, questions were being called after them.

"Hey, Lissa, what are you doing Saturday night?" a male voice called out, followed by several whistles and wolf-howls.

Once more David Andrews was on the screen. "Well that's it, Robin. The Royal Wedding is off and apparently they've chosen not to answer any questions from the floor."

The picture switched back to the in-station newscaster, and Lucas turned off the TV.

Morgan continued to look at the blank screen. Was it really over between them? Melissa had said it was. Now they'd both gone on TV and said it was, but was she secretly hoping for a reconciliation?

Emmie had acted resigned about her broken engagement, too. But all the time she'd been plotting to win Robert back, playing them both for fools.

"I wonder what Melissa does have planned for Saturday night?" Luc's voice broke the silence. "Why don't you give her a call?"

"What?"

"Give her a call. Ask her out."

"You want me to ask Melly out?"

"Sure, why not? Her engagement's off and I think you two would make a good couple."

"Listen, Luc, your sister's a very attractive woman, but she's not my type." *Right, pal, and the sun doesn't rise in the east.*

"How can you be sure unless you go out with her at least once?"

"I took her to McCoy's last week. Does that count?"

"And . . ." Lucas prompted.

"And nothing. Like I told you, not my type."

"That's not *really* a date." Lucas dismissed Morgan's objection. "It needs to be longer. Like dinner, a movie, then a walk on the beach." He nudged Morgan with his elbow.

McCoy's had been enough of a date for Morgan to know that he was interested. He had enjoyed talking to Melly. She was one of the few people who had seemed to understand how he felt about architecture. Buildings were such a functional part of people's lives, they seldom stopped to consider the artistic side of them. But Melly had understood.

He wondered if deli sandwiches, knock-knock and

elephant jokes, and sharing a couch for the night would better fit Luc's idea of a date? Probably not. "Luc get your racquet. Let's play."

"Hey, we could even make it a double date, just like the old days."

Morgan laughed. "You're going to let me get into the backseat of your car with your sister?"

"Well . . . not exactly like the old days. I think we've both outgrown necking in the car. Or at least I have."

Morgan had outgrown it, too. Hadn't he? The memory of last Friday came crashing in on him. It was just a kiss, he reminded himself. They hadn't been necking—they hadn't been able to get close enough to do it right with the bucket seats, for heaven's sake!

His voice was strained when he answered Luc. "A double date sounds fine, but I'll pick my own lady. All right?"

"Fine, but I think you should seriously consider asking Melissa."

Morgan's eyes narrowed suspiciously. "Did Melly put you up to this?"

Lucas looked surprised, then his expression gradually shifted to self-satisfied. "No. No, she didn't. But there must be a reason you would suspect she might have." He walked over to the couch and picked up his racquet. "Let's hit the court."

Morgan was angry at himself for sparking Luc's suspicions. It was hard enough fighting his own desires for Melly. He didn't need Luc pushing him toward her as well.

* * *

The phone was ringing Saturday afternoon when Melissa entered the apartment. "Hold your horses," she muttered, setting her laundry basket next to the door and running over to grab the phone.

"Lissa, I was beginning to think you weren't home."

"I just got back from the laundry room. Some of us do our own laundry, Lucas."

"Mom offered. I didn't ask."

"So what can I do for you? Or did you call so we could rehash the infamous laundry debate?"

"I called because I need a favor."

Melissa sighed. "What is it this time?"

"I've got a few people over here for a party and I underestimated how thirsty they'd be."

"That's not like you, Luc."

"So what do you say? Will you pick up some more beer and soda for me and bring them by?"

"Guess I'd better. I wouldn't want you to lose your Host With The Most status."

"Thanks, Lissa. I owe you one. See you soon."

"You're welcome," she said automatically even though Luc had already hung up his phone.

She went into her room and changed into clean blue jeans and a red silk blouse topped by a plaid blazer.

She stopped at a store on the way to Luc's Mission Bay Condominium and picked up the drinks he'd asked for. When she got to Luc's she went in the back door.

Even with the kitchen door closed, she could hear

music, talking, and laughter coming from the other room. She carried the cans in and put what would fit into the refrigerator.

Picking up what was left, she opened the door into the walk-in pantry, just as Lucas came in from the front part of the condo.

"Hi, Luc. The fridge is full. I'll just put these extras in the pantry."

"Lissa . . . wait! Just put them on the counter."

But she was already in the pantry—eye-to-eye with a full shelf of beer and soda. She looked back over her shoulder at her brother.

Luc shrugged and smiled sheepishly.

"You're not running out of drinks."

"It doesn't hurt to be well stocked."

"Well stocked? Lucas, there's enough here for three parties!"

"This is a very thirsty group." He took the cans from her and set them on the counter. "I appreciate your helping out, Lissa." Taking her by the hand, he started back to the party. "Since you're here, why don't you come out and say hi."

Before she could protest, she found herself looking around Luc's crowded living room. She estimated there were about thirty people, some who looked vaguely familiar but no one she could put a name to. Until the crowd shifted slightly and she saw Morgan.

He was leaning nonchalantly against the wall, a woman on his right and one in front. Though the two women seemed to be having a great time of it, Morgan looked bored. Although he was talking and even laughed at something one of the women said to him, that extra spark of animation was missing.

Of course that didn't stop Melissa's heartbeat from kicking into overdrive as she looked at him.

"You remember Sherri Harris, don't you?" Luc asked. "She lived around the corner from us. She recognized you on the news Tuesday and asked about you."

Sherri Harris—the name immediately clicked with the pretty brunette standing on Morgan's right. And of course, as he talked, Lucas was leading her straight toward them.

Luc handled the introductions. The other woman's name was Gail Farmer. Morgan acknowledged Melissa's presence with a nod.

The women were full of questions about Brian and his teammates.

Melissa didn't mind talking about Brian. It kept her from having to think about Morgan, standing only a few feet away—but it might as well have been miles for all that he seemed to notice her. He was busily looking around the room, not even pretending to listen to their conversation.

Until Gail asked Melissa in a stage whisper, "So, tell us . . . how is he in the sack?"

Out of the corner of her eye, Melissa saw Morgan's body tense. When she looked at him, his eyes were blazing angrily. Why did he look angry at her? *She* hadn't asked the question.

She looked back at Gail. "Don't you think that question is a bit personal?"

"Maybe. But guys compare notes, you know. I'll

bet Brian's teammates know all about your indoor sports skills.''

"Speaking of indoor sports, Gail. Why don't we dance?'' Lucas came to Melissa's rescue.

She could feel Morgan's eyes on her but refused to look at him.

"Don't mind Gail. She always was too outspoken for her own good. Right, Morgan?'' Sherri said.

"You've got that right.''

Sherri changed the subject, filling Melissa in on news of some of the other people from the old neighborhood gang.

Luc came back without Gail as the next song started and asked Sherri to dance, leaving Melissa alone with Morgan.

"I don't remember you being in our high school class.'' Morgan spoke to her for the first time since her arrival.

"Is this a reunion?''

"Of sorts.''

"Well, I wasn't in your class. Luc called and asked me to bring some extra drinks over.''

"I'm surprised you and Luc didn't come up with a more original excuse.''

"Excuse? Excuse for what?''

"For the two of us to be thrown together.''

"You think Luc and I planned this?'' A picture of the full shelf of drinks flashed in her mind. Had Luc planned for her to be thrown together with Morgan? She also remembered the way he'd taken Sherri and Gail away. Just wait until she had him alone.

"Tell me this wasn't a setup.''

"Boy, what an ego. If you think I've got nothing better to do on a Saturday afternoon than chase after you, Morgan Edwards, you are sadly mistaken!" Like the two loads of laundry she had sitting at home waiting for her to put them away.

"I told Luc Tuesday night that I wouldn't ask you out. Wednesday he calls with the details of this party. I agreed to come and then *coincidentally* who should appear? Little sister." His voice was loaded with sarcasm.

"Luc asked you to ask me out?" She was going to strangle him!

"Yes."

"As a favor, I suppose."

"No. He mistakenly thought I might be interested." His comment cut her to the quick. "Well, I certainly hope you put him straight on that account."

"I thought I had until you showed up."

"I'll talk to Luc and make sure it doesn't happen again."

"I'd appreciate it."

"Oh, I'll just bet you would." God, she hated this cold, icy mask he was wearing. Or maybe this was the real Morgan—maybe the warm, caring friend had been the mask.

"Melly, women on the rebound are bad news."

"Why?"

"They're desperate and cling to the first gullible male they can get their claws into."

"Not a very flattering picture." Was that the problem? Was he running scared because he thought she was going to sink her claws into him? "The other day when I suggested that the two of us could start seeing each other, I didn't mean you would jump right in where Brian left off. I just thought it might be nice if we spent some time together, got to know each other better."

"And I think I made my feelings on the matter very clear."

"You did. But there's something you're overlooking. I'm not on the rebound. Not really. I was going to call the engagement off myself, remember?"

"You *planned* to call it off. But would you really have gone through with it?"

"Of course."

"You don't think Marshall would have talked you out of it?"

"No. I'd made up my mind and I would have stuck with it."

"We'll never know for sure, will we?"

"Why don't you believe me?" It was strange how he didn't seem to believe her. He had no reason to doubt her. So what was causing this blind spot?

"Oh, I believe that you really think you would have stuck to your plan. But when it came right down to walking away from the fame and fortune of being Mrs. Brian Marshall, I don't think you'd have done it."

"Then you don't know me very well."

"I never claimed to." He shrugged.

"But you're making broad generalizations and speculations about my behavior."

"All right, I apologize. Maybe you are the exception to the rule."

"But you don't think so?"

"No."

"And you're not interested in finding out if you're right?"

"No." He met her gaze straight on. But where was the warmth, caring, and compassion she was so used to seeing in his eyes—not to mention the passion and desire she'd seen there the day he'd kissed her.

"Tell me . . . when did this total lack of interest start?"

"I'm sorry, but there never was any interest," he denied flatly.

"You took me to McCoy's after I'd argued with Brian."

"To cheer you up. I would have done the same for anyone."

"You kissed me."

"You asked. And as you pointed out, I *had* promised."

"Maybe, but I'll bet you wouldn't kiss me again if I asked."

"I only promised once."

"And I'll bet you wouldn't take me to McCoy's right now, either."

"You're right."

"I'd like to know why." She knew she was pushing her luck, but if he would do the same for anyone, why was she now excluded?

"Because it's the middle of a party."

"You've never left a party early?"

He grinned wickedly. "Not to go to McCoy's."

"And if I asked you to leave early with me . . ." she paused. "And *not* go to McCoy's, would you?"

"No." He shook his head.

"I appreciate your honesty. Thanks." Without saying good-bye she turned and walked away. She forced herself to walk slowly when she longed to run as fast and as far from Morgan as she could get.

The caterers had arrived and were setting up in the kitchen as she passed through. She smiled politely and let herself out the back door.

Luc caught up with her as she reached her car. "Lissa, where are you going?"

"Home." She started to open her car door, but in her anger and frustration she couldn't get the key into the lock.

When Luc easily performed the task for her, she had reached the boiling point. "Lucas Ellison, if you ever set me up like this again, I'll . . . I'll . . ."

"You'll what? Short-sheet my bed, put salt in my sugar bowl, sew my pant legs shut. Aren't we getting a bit old for those kinds of things now?"

"You're right. We are too old for sibling practical jokes and if you want to get any older, stay out of my personal life!"

"I thought you had a crush on Morgan. Now that your engagement is off I thought it might be nice if—"

"Stop thinking so much, Luc." She got into her car and took off.

She still didn't understand Morgan's aversion to her. What had caused it and why it continued. It was so confusing!

But the facts remained—he wasn't interested, even though her last question had almost been a clear-cut offer to go to bed with him.

Honesty. She had thanked him for his honesty! And he had lied. He would have loved to have left with her, even if it was for nothing more than ice cream—although the "more" she had implied would have been very welcome, too.

But how could he be sure it was really him she wanted? He didn't want to be just a convenience to step in and fill the space Brian's breaking up with her had left in her life. And he didn't want to be a decoy to lure him back, either.

If only he could trust her. If only he could believe that the interest she seemed to be showing in him was really for him and not stemming from ulterior motives.

Gail's question about Marshall's performance in the bedroom had struck him like a knife. He still hated the thought of the two of them together. It wasn't like him to be jealous, but then again, it wasn't like him to be running scared, either.

But lately he'd been doing both.

He looked around the room at the other women. Gail was definitely off the list, but that still left a number of others he could ask out.

But the undeniable truth slammed into him full force. He didn't want another woman. He *only* wanted Melly.

Even if he was just a substitute or a decoy, it was better than nothing.

Even with Emmie, he had maintained his pride. He'd never let her see how much she'd hurt him. Where had his pride gone? Something had obviously driven it down, but what could possibly be strong enough to do that?

SEVEN

Melissa put the last suitcase in the trunk of her car and closed the lid. She hoped she hadn't forgotten anything.

"Ready?" Carol asked.

"As ready as I'll ever be."

The two of them got into the car. "Carol, are you sure this is a good idea?" Melissa had been vacillating since Sunday, when her mother had announced they had all been invited to spend the next weekend at Mr. and Mrs. Edwards' house in Palm Springs. The invitation had included Melissa bringing a friend.

"All I remember saying was that it couldn't hurt. Do you know yet if Morgan is even going to be there?"

"He'll be there. He and Luc are driving up tonight, too."

111

"Did Luc tell him you were going?"

"I don't know. But with everybody else knowing, I would imagine Morgan knows I'll be there."

"If he knows and he's still going, he must not be trying to avoid you."

"Or it might just mean he's completely indifferent to my presence."

"Maybe. But like I told you the other day, I think this coolness of his is just an act."

"I hope we can find out what's behind it this weekend."

"Me, too. You know I was thinking at work today and I wondered if maybe this whole weekend wasn't Morgan's idea."

"I don't think so, Carol. If he wanted to see me he's got my phone number and he knows where I live. He wouldn't have to arrange a weekend at his parents' house."

"Well . . . it was just a thought." Carol shrugged. "We're never going to get there if you don't start the car."

"Right." Melissa turned the key. She began to put the car in reverse, then stopped. "Did I turn off the coffee maker?"

"I did."

"The trash . . ."

"Lissa, the trash is out, the plants were watered, the thermostat has been turned down, the stove is off, and the electric curlers and blowdryers are in the suitcases. Now, let's go. The man of my dreams may be waiting for me in Palm Springs and you're keeping me from him," she teased.

Carol had gone steady with Steve through her junior year in high school. When he'd gone out of state to college, the relationship had tapered off. Since then, she didn't have trouble getting dates, but like Melissa until she'd met Brian, hadn't had much luck finding anyone she wanted to make a long-term commitment to.

The drive went smoothly and they had little trouble following the directions Melissa had gotten from her mother. They pulled into the wide circular driveway in front of the sprawling single-story Spanish-style house and parked behind her parents' car. Frank and Jean had driven themselves down because they planned to spend the whole week with Mitch and Evelyn Edwards.

"How did the guys get here so quickly?" Carol drew Melissa's attention to Morgan's car, which was parked next to the garage.

"I don't know. Maybe they left earlier than they'd planned to or maybe they didn't stop for dinner."

Melissa and Carol got the suitcases out of the car and headed for the porch.

The front door opened. "They're here. I told you I heard a car, Evelyn."

By the time the two of them got into the house, Frank, Jean, Evelyn, Lucas, and Morgan had joined Mitch in the entry hall. The interior decor of the home continued the Southwest theme promised by the outside.

"This can't be little Melissa!" Mitch took her hand. "She's certainly grown up to be a beauty.

Don't you think so, Morgan? Bet you keep a loaded shotgun handy, Frank.''

Melissa blushed, uncomfortable with the attention Mitch had called to her and glad he hadn't pushed his son for an answer to his question.

Mitch and Evelyn Edwards were much as she remembered them from ten years ago. Morgan got his height and dark hair from his father, but his blue eyes were a perfect match of his mother's.

When Melissa looked in Morgan's direction, her eyes locked with his across the room. Neither of them spoke or acknowledged each other in any way.

After the rest of the greetings were exchanged and Carol was introduced, Evelyn offered to show Carol and Melissa to their rooms.

As Melissa picked up her luggage, Morgan was at her side. ''I'll take that for you.'' He reached for her suitcase.

His hand was warm against hers as it slid into the handle of her suitcase. Reluctantly, she released her grip and left it to him.

''Thank you.'' She gave him a small, uncertain smile.

He reciprocated by flashing her one of his heart-stoppingly sexy grins.

Melissa and Carol's rooms were side by side, on the front of the house facing the street. Morgan left her suitcase inside the door to her room and then headed back down the hallway.

''I'll leave you to freshen up. When you're ready, join the rest of us in the family room. Go back to the entry hall and then head straight for the back of the house. You can't miss it.''

''Thank you, Mrs. Edwards.''

''Evelyn, please.''

''Evelyn.''

''What a nice lady,'' Carol remarked after Evelyn left. ''She'll make a much better mother-in-law than Beverly Marshall.''

''Carol!''

''Well, she will,'' Carol insisted. ''I'm going to go get cleaned up.''

Carol went off to her own room. Melissa closed the door behind her.

Carol had a point, Evelyn would probably make a wonderful mother-in-law. Of course an important part of the wife/mother-in-law relationship was how the husband handled his relationship with them.

Why was she worrying about it? Having Evelyn for a mother-in-law meant having Morgan for a husband. A nice thought, but it was a pretty big jump from helping with her luggage to marrying her.

She had resolved to keep her imagination under control this weekend. This wasn't a very auspicious start! Darn Carol, for mentioning Evelyn's mother-in-law potential in the first place!

She went into the bathroom. A shower always felt so good after a long drive, even in cool weather.

Carol was waiting for her when she stepped back into the bedroom. ''So far so good,'' she said.

''What?''

''Morgan carried your suitcase.''

"He was just being polite, Carol. Luc carried yours. Any possibilities there?"

Carol wrinkled up her nose. "No thanks, I wouldn't take that heartbreaker gift-wrapped."

"I don't know about now, but in the past Morgan's track record was as bad as Luc's."

"He's changed," Carol said with complete confidence.

Melissa laughed. "How do you know? You just met him, for heaven's sake."

"I just know."

"I'm not going to argue the point with you, but I'm not going to get my hopes up, either."

Carol was thoughtful for a moment. "Guess that's a good idea. Men are so unpredictable!"

Later in the evening, Melissa was even more convinced Carol had hit the nail on the head.

Unpredictable was a perfect description of Morgan's behavior. He was being a perfect gentleman but acting as if they'd just met for the first time.

There was none of the judging or criticizing he'd shown when she was engaged to Brian, and none of the cold aloofness he'd displayed since the morning she'd told him her engagement was off. But also missing was the comfortable friendship they'd shared at times.

Of course, it all might have been for the benefit of their parents.

With four men present, inevitably the conversation drifted to sports.

"Speaking of football . . ." Lucas turned to

Melissa. "You still have my Sports Edition Trivial Pursuit cards."

"They're at Brian's. I'll get them for you next week."

Morgan shifted in his chair. "Why don't you call Marshall and pick them up yourself, Luc?"

"Why?" Luc's question was the same one Melissa had. Carol, too, if the puzzled look on her face was anything to go by.

"Don't you think it might be a little awkward for Melly to see Marshall?"

"Their breakup was an 'amicable agreement,' " Luc quoted Brian's words from the press conference.

"But still . . ." Morgan persisted.

"Lissa, if it's a problem for you, I'll take care of it myself, all right?"

"There's no problem at all, Luc. *I* borrowed the cards and *I'll* get them back for you."

Morgan was frowning. She wasn't sure why.

Did the thought of her seeing Brian upset him? Why should it if he had no interest in her? And if he was interested, then why didn't he say so? She wished she could read his mind.

When she curled up in bed for the night, Morgan's behavior was still puzzling her. She couldn't stop thinking about him. He was starting to haunt her thoughts, day and night, as he'd done when she was a teenager.

She was also no closer to understanding the intensity and magnitude of her physical reaction to him, either. What she had felt for Brian was certainly nothing like this, and she'd been on the verge of marrying him.

She plumped up her pillow and tried to put Morgan out of her mind. Why, oh, why had she agreed to this weekend? She could have come up with any number of legitimate excuses.

So why hadn't she used one of them? Had she come because she believed she had a chance with Morgan? Did she have a chance with him or was she just fooling herself?

It wasn't like her to go chasing after a man—especially since Morgan had stated on two separate occasions that he wasn't interested in her.

But if he wasn't interested, why did he seem displeased with the thought of her seeing Brian? Her mind continued tormenting her with unanswerable questions, until in the early morning hours sleep finally came.

Morgan also had trouble getting to sleep. He'd tried his best to reestablish the easy rapport that had existed between him and Melly the afternoon he'd taken her out for a sundae, but it didn't seem to be working. She seemed to be holding back.

Of course, what did he expect after the way he'd been treating her since her engagement was canceled? He'd been a real bastard. Did he expect her to just ignore everything he'd said and done?

Plus they'd had an audience this evening—both sets of parents, Lucas and Carol.

Maybe this weekend hadn't been such a good idea after all. But it had seemed important to him to get her away from where she might run into Marshall or any of the reporters Lucas said kept showing up at the store or her apartment.

He'd wanted her away from anything that would remind her of her ex-fiancé. Someplace where he could wipe the slate clean and start over. Now, thanks to Luc, she would be seeing Marshall next week. The thought of it was killing him.

He almost wanted to volunteer to do the errand for her, but what reason could he give for offering?

He could level with her. Tell her about Emmie and how he didn't want to be placed in the same position again. But if she was like Emmie, he would be playing right into her hands, and if she wasn't, she wouldn't be very flattered knowing he didn't trust her.

No, he didn't think she was the type of woman who would let herself get involved with a man who didn't trust her. She had too much self-respect.

There had to be another way to put their relationship back on its old footing so they could pick up where they'd left off in his car. . . . There just had to be.

He had been going to spend the day with her tomorrow, but maybe this weekend wasn't the time to be working on a relationship? Maybe he should wait until *after* she'd seen Marshall next week?

Melissa couldn't believe how late she slept in the next morning. Of course, she'd fallen asleep later than usual and it hadn't been the most peaceful sleep she'd ever had.

The reason for her disturbed sleep sat across the breakfast table from her, looking fully rested—that rat!

Evelyn announced her ideas for the day's activities: a trip to the Palm Springs Desert Museum and a ride on the Aerial Tramway to the top of San Jacinto—an ascent of over eight thousand feet in eighteen minutes, passing through five climatic zones in the process.

"Frank and I thought we'd hit the golf course this morning," Mitch said.

"And Luc and I have a court time at the racquet club, Mom."

"Guess that leaves the four of us ladies."

Melissa was both relieved and disappointed she wouldn't be around Morgan all day. Relieved because she would be able to enjoy the local sites without being on her guard every second, but disappointed with Morgan's choice to spend the day playing racquetball with Lucas. It seemed clear pursuing her was not high on his list of things-to-do-this-weekend—if it was even on the list at all.

After breakfast, Melissa went back to her room to get her purse. She was about to walk out the door, when she thought she heard a VW engine start up.

Going over to the window, she pulled back the curtain, opened up the miniblinds, and looked out. Morgan was backing a yellow VW out one of the three doors of his parents' garage.

Carol entered the room and came to stand by her side. "What's up?"

"That's Morgan's old VW."

"And he's still got it? Even though he has a Ferrari?"

"It appears so." Morgan headed out of the driveway and down the street.

"It either has investment potential for him, or this guy's got a strong sentimental streak."

"I wonder." Melissa closed the blinds and curtains. "Maybe the interest he showed in me initially was just out of a sense of nostalgia."

"The interest you speak of, being the kiss?"

"Yes."

"Come off it, Lissa. Nostalgia is not what makes men kiss women. If it was, think how devastating that would be to the fashion and cosmetic industries."

"You're right. But it's driving me nuts not knowing if he only kissed me because I asked or if it was for another reason."

"Lissa, you've got to be patient."

"Easy for you to say."

Carol laughed. "Hardly! Do you know how difficult it is to live with you in this mood you've been in lately?"

"Pretty tough?"

"Close to impossible, but what are best friends for?"

The four women got back to the house around four that afternoon. Morgan and Luc were sitting at the kitchen table drinking lemonade.

"Ah, the sightseeing expedition has returned," Luc announced.

"How was it?" Morgan asked, looking at Melissa.

"Fine. And your racquetball game?" she returned politely.

"All right."

"All right?" Luc interjected. "This guy wiped up the court with me! That's twice now."

"Would you and Carol like to take in a movie tonight?" Morgan asked.

Melissa didn't think Carol would mind changing their plans to go dancing at one of the local nightclubs. But Morgan had put his game with Luc above spending time with her during the day and her bruised ego refused to let her give in to him now. Besides, he could have asked this morning. "Actually, we've already made plans for the evening."

Their eyes were locked. Melissa held her breath, waiting for his response. Would his politeness slip with disappointment or irritation—or had the invitation only been a polite gesture to begin with? It might even have been Luc's idea.

"Perhaps another time then?" He looked down at his glass, picked it up, and took a drink.

"Perhaps."

The look Luc sent her left no doubt in her mind that he thought she was making a bad move.

Had it been a bad move? Had this been a peace offering from Morgan? Should she have set aside all her doubts and accepted?

"Any sign of your father yet?" Evelyn asked, breaking the tense silence that had come over the room.

"No."

"I hope he doesn't forget he's supposed to barbecue."

Morgan and Luc ended up manning the grill. Mitch and Frank came in just as the rest of them were sitting down to eat.

During dinner, Mitch recounted their golf game stroke by stroke and filled them in on all the news of everyone he and Frank had run into.

"Both Reggie and Harv have new grandchildren. Of course, they had several dozen pictures on hand. And the kids are only a few months old! Made me feel a little left out . . . again." He looked pointedly at Morgan. "How 'bout you, Frank?"

"Grandchildren would be nice, but I think Jean's more impatient about it than I am. When Melissa announced her engagement, she was more excited about the prospect of being a grandmother than being the mother of the bride."

Morgan's fork clattered to the table.

"Um . . . Dad," Luc cut into Frank and Mitch's conversation.

Frank stopped talking, but Mitch didn't seem to take the hint. "Maybe we should get Morgan and Melissa together. What do you say, guys?" He looked from one to the other of them.

Melissa could feel the blood draining from her face. She wanted to crawl underneath the table. It was that or die of embarrassment . . . or both!

Morgan's father continued. "Frank, Jean, Evelyn, and I have waited long enough for grandchildren."

"Now, Mitch, stop teasing," Evelyn said.

"Who's teasing? I'm serious."

"You seem to have forgotten about Frank's shotgun," Jean teased.

"Well, of course I meant he should marry her first! She's gorgeous, great figure, comes from a good family . . . what more could he ask for?"

"I think that's enough." Morgan's voice was cold and hard.

Melissa glanced at him through the cover of her lashes. He was looking down the table at his father, the hard planes of his face tightened in anger, his eyes flashing. Did he find the thought of marrying her so repulsive?

"Excuse me," she murmured. Standing up and then walking quickly from the room, she made her escape.

Once in her room, she washed her face in the bathroom and was going to lie down on the bed when there was a knock on the door.

She expected it to be Carol and was shocked to find Morgan in the hallway when she opened the door.

"May I come in?"

She couldn't imagine why he'd want to, but she stepped aside and let him in, closing the door behind him.

"Are you all right?" he asked, turning back to face her, his blue eyes full of concern.

She nodded, uncomfortably aware of the intimacy of the two of them alone in her bedroom.

"Dad got a little carried away. I'm sorry."

"He was just teasing. I shouldn't have taken it so

much to heart." She knew she shouldn't have, but it had been impossible not to, as she'd pictured herself, Morgan, and their children piling out of the family minivan for a visit with Grandpa and Grandma Edwards. Not to mention the thoughts of the physical act necessary to start each child in the first place.

"It was still in unexcusably poor taste. Especially with all you've just been through with your engagement."

"I don't think he meant it maliciously."

"No, I'm sure he didn't. It's an old argument between the two of us. He usually reminds me how old I was when he was at my age now. He just can't seem to accept the idea that I may never settle down and get married. I've gotten used to his remarks and they don't bother me much anymore, but I'm so very sorry he chose to bring it up in front of company and drag you into it this time."

His hand came up slowly and stroked her cheek. He started to drop his arm back to his side, but then reached out and pulled her to him.

Melissa let him hold her, his chin resting on the top of her head, his arms wrapped tightly around her.

"You turned so white, I was worried about you."

She closed her eyes, letting the warmth and security of him wash over her. She remembered the look of anger and disgust on his face at the table. Could it all have been directed at his father rather than at the thought of being paired with her as she'd thought at the time?

A small spark of hope flared within her. He obviously cared a little, he'd come to make sure she was all right. But how much did he care . . . and in what way? He'd just said he might never settle down and get married—so even if he cared, where did that leave her?

He had been so adamant in his rejection of her at Luc's party, she didn't feel she could completely discount what he'd said. But something in his attitude had changed—or was it just wishful thinking on her part?

Morgan loosened his hold and leaned back to look down at her. He looked deeply into her eyes, searching—for what she didn't know.

His gaze dropped to her lips and her thoughts flew to the memory of his kiss. She longed for a repeat performance. Her tongue slid along her bottom lip to ease the tingling sensation building up there.

"Well . . . if you're sure you're all right, I'll leave you alone." Morgan pulled back, his hands caressing her shoulders one more time before he released her completely.

"I'm fine." Not completely true, but she *was* over the turmoil Mitch's remarks had caused.

"Would you like me to send Carol in?"

"That won't be necessary. Really, I'm fine." She smiled to reassure him.

The room seemed very empty after Morgan left it.

Damn, why hadn't he kissed her? She'd wanted him to, he'd seen it in her eyes. What had held him back? His fears about Marshall?

This is not like you, pal, this uncertainty. Even if Marshall was still in the running, maybe he should just push ahead and give him a run for his money like he'd been planning before the wedding had been called off.

He'd felt confident enough to take him on before. The similarities in the breakups between Emmie and Robert and Melissa and Brian had knocked him off track for a while. But he was ready now. . . .

Luc had found out where Melly and Carol were planning to go and had made reservations for the two of them. She would have some space and time to calm down from the fiasco at dinner and then he'd make his move.

He wondered at the strength of her reaction to his father's suggesting the two of them get married and provide grandchildren. Had her reaction merely been embarrassment at the intimate nature of the suggestion or had his behavior over the last few weeks truly succeeded in killing any feelings she'd had for him?

Maybe *her* experience with Brian had made her as unready for marriage as *his* experience with Emmie had made him. Surprisingly, he realized the thought of settling down and getting married didn't sound quite as improbable as it once had.

For him at least . . . but what about Melly? She was recovering from a broken engagement and she was only twenty-four. Marriage might not be in her plans for the immediate future. He wouldn't push that issue, but he was going to pursue *her*.

Funny how he could almost picture what their children would look like. . . .

EIGHT

"You should have heard him give his father hell! Boy, he really let him have it. And I think it's so cute the way he calls you Melly. I thought maybe after he'd gone in to talk to you, you'd reconsider his invitation to the movies." Carol had been on one track ever since the two of them had left the Edwards' house and headed for the Desert Chic.

"Carol, I told you he just apologized for what his father had said and that was that."

"He held you."

"But he didn't even try to kiss me."

"Maybe he was afraid to after you'd turned down his invitation. Maybe he wants to take things slowly."

"And maybe he's just not interested. He came right out and said he didn't know if he would ever settle down and get married. Is this where I turn?" Melissa changed the subject.

"Yes, this is it."

Melissa turned into the parking lot. The attendant opened the passenger door for Carol, then came around and let Melissa out.

They entered the club and Melissa felt like she'd walked through a time warp. Everything but the music and the other patrons looked right out of an old Valentino movie. Over the dance floor was a mock tent top, but the rest of the ceiling was dark blue with twinkling lights to give the effect of a starry desert night.

A waiter, dressed like a desert sheik, led them to their table and took their drink order.

"How did you find out about this club?" Melissa asked Carol.

"One of my student's mothers recommended it."

Melissa watched the couples dancing. The loud music and tailored designer clothes was a strong contrast to the peaceful decor and flowing costumes of the employees, but somehow it all worked.

She hadn't realized how much she'd needed a night out. With all that had been going on in her life the past few weeks, she hadn't taken any time to just relax and have a good time.

She looked around at the other tables. There were groups of women, groups of men, and couples. Looking up, she saw a second level of tables which was also starting to fill up.

The waiter returned with their drinks.

"I'd like to take him home with me," Carol teased as he walked away.

"Think he'd give up his job here to move to San Diego?"

"You have a point. But I could always move here."

Melissa laughed. Her laughter died when she noticed two newcomers being seated at a table on the other side of the room, but in their line of vision. "Did you happen to mention to Luc or Morgan that we were coming here?"

"No, of course not," Carol sounded offended.

Melissa nodded in their direction. "Guess they decided not to go to the movies. With all the night spots in Palm Springs, I wonder why they picked this one—?"

"Oops, Lissa, I just thought of something," Carol interrupted her.

"What?"

"Luc walked into the living room just as I finished making reservations. He tried to get me to tell him where we were going, but I wouldn't. I didn't think about it at the time, but the phone had one of those redial buttons and he stayed in the room after I left."

Melissa sighed. "I'll bet he called and made reservations for the two of them. And after I threatened his very life if he didn't stay out of mine!"

"Do you want to go somewhere else or back to the house?"

"No, I'm not going to let the two of them ruin our evening out."

Despite her resolve, it was hard to ignore Morgan's presence. Every time she accepted an offer to dance, she couldn't stop herself from looking over to see if Morgan noticed—a thrill of pleasure shooting through her if he was looking and a twinge of disappointment if he wasn't.

She kept waiting for him to come over and ask her to dance. When he didn't, she began to wonder if his being there could really be a coincidence after all. Had he and Luc just decided to go out on the town? Were they here to meet women?

She kept careful watch on how often he danced and with whom. So far he hadn't danced with the same woman more than once. That was encouraging—wasn't it? *You're crazy to torture yourself this way!* she reprimanded herself. *Just ignore the guy.*

But it only got harder as the evening moved on.

Especially when two of the women Morgan and Luc danced with moved their purses and drinks to the guys' table. Similar pairing up was going on all around them. She and Carol had had several offers themselves, which they'd refused.

The redhead sitting next to Morgan kept putting her hand underneath the table and it was driving Melissa nuts. The woman either had the itchiest knee in the room or she was putting some major moves on Morgan.

The brunette wasn't any more subtle; she was all over Lucas.

"Let's visit the ladies' room," Melissa said to Carol. It was that or do something she'd regret.

Out of sight was not out of mind in this case, but it was a relief to be out of the room.

Carol fluffed up her hair and took out her lipstick.

"Why don't you just go over and ask Morgan to dance, Lissa?"

"If he wants to dance with me, he'll ask. Besides, it looks like he'll probably be leaving soon."

"You don't really think he'll leave with that woman, do you?"

"It looks like it."

"After he went through all the trouble of following you here?"

"We don't know for a fact they followed us here. Even if Luc did use the redial on the phone to find out where we were going, it doesn't mean Morgan was part of it. Remember how Luc tricked me into showing up at his party? Morgan might have been just as surprised to see us as we were to see him."

"I suppose."

Melissa put her brush back in her purse and turned to Carol. "Ready to head back to the table?"

"Sure."

The door opened and the two women who had been sitting with Morgan and Lucas walked in. Melissa opened her purse and took her brush back out.

"Lissa?" Carol asked after the women had passed through the lounge into the room beyond.

"I think your lipstick could use more freshening up, Carol," Melissa said with a wink.

Carol leaned over toward her and whispered, "That sparkle in your eye means trouble. What are you up to?"

"Just follow my lead," she whispered back.

A few minutes later the women were back. They

came over to the mirror and began freshening their makeup.

"Valerie, why don't you take my keys now," the brunette who had been draping herself over Lucas said. "You and Morgan can have my car and our hotel room for the night."

"You're not coming back tonight?"

"I'm sure Lukey can make the hours fly by."

Lukey? Melissa had to bite the inside of her lip to keep from laughing out loud.

"Think he'll let you drive his Ferrari, Jade?"

It was the opening Melissa'd been waiting for and she jumped on it. "Excuse me. Was the blond man you're with driving a red Ferrari?"

"Yes, it's red."

"Well . . . I don't mean to intrude on your plans, but woman to woman," she lowered her voice conspiratorially, "I think you should know the car isn't his."

"Not his?" the redhead who'd been chasing Morgan asked.

"No. It belongs to a friend of his."

"How do you know?" the brunette asked, suspiciously.

"I know the owner of the car."

"Do you know Lukey?"

"We've met."

"Well . . . what does he drive?" The look on her face clearly showed it had better be something comparable.

Not knowing how the other woman would classify a restored 1966 Triumph Spitfire, she feigned ignorance. "I don't know, but this morning I saw the dark-haired guy with him driving a VW bug."

The two women looked horrified. "A VW?" they asked in unison.

"Yes. Remember, Carol? You were with me."

"Yes. I saw him, too."

"You're sure it was Morgan?" the redhead asked.

"It was the dark-haired one. Is his name Morgan? Does he look like a Morgan to you?" she asked Carol. Melissa stood up to go.

Carol followed. "Morgan? I think it suits him."

"Have a nice night, ladies."

Carol giggled as they headed back to their table. "*Lukey* would blow a fuse if he knew you'd ruined his after-hours entertainment."

"Hey, I did him a favor. Those women were obviously more interested in fast cars and money than they were in Luc and Morgan. Can you believe how quickly they backed off when I told them I'd seen Morgan driving a VW? Heck, I'd take him driving a lawn tractor!"

"You and a lot of other women. You really should consider going over there and asking him to dance."

They sat back down at their table. "Carol, I've put my pride and ego on the line for him twice already. The next move is his."

"She keeps glancing this way, pal."

Morgan pulled his eyes away from Melly and turned to look at Luc. "So?"

"So . . . I'm sure she's noticed you staring at her.

Why don't you go ask her to dance and put the two of you out of your misery?''

Good question. But he didn't have a good answer. For several hours he'd watched the men come and go from Melly and Carol's table. He hated watching her dance with them, talk with them, but he sure loved watching her send them on their way—especially the tanned, blond Marshall types.

And he loved the way her eyes kept turning in his direction . . . Especially when Valerie and Jade had been with them. He couldn't figure out why the women had taken off so abruptly after coming back from the ladies' room. But it didn't matter, he hadn't planned on responding to Valerie's come-hither looks or her hand running up his thigh, anyway.

Luc continued. ''If you didn't mean to make a move on her, why did we go through all the trouble of finding out where they were going and then showing up?''

''I just wanted to be sure they were safe. They are my parents' guests.''

''Yeah, right.'' Luc laughed.

Morgan noticed a guy approaching Melissa. She'd already danced with him several times before. Maybe Luc was right. Maybe it was time for him to make his move. It wasn't like him to drag his feet like this. He usually picked his prey and moved in for the kill.

He was too late for this dance, but he made sure he was there waiting for her when she returned to the table. He took her by the hand before she had a chance to sit down and led her out onto the dance floor.

Almost as if he'd read Morgan's thoughts, the D.J. slowed the music down.

Morgan took Melissa into his arms. Once again he marveled at how wonderful she felt. "Having a good time?" *Brilliant conversationalist, buddy! That's sure to charm her.*

"Yes. Are you?" Was there a hint of jealousy in her voice?

"Now I am."

Her eyes opened wide in surprise. Beautiful emerald green, reflecting the lights that blinked and flashed around them.

Melly was tense and there was a wary look in her eyes.

"I noticed you watching me." He pulled her closer.

"I have not." She started to pull away from him, but he held her close.

"Don't deny it. Even Luc noticed."

"Then you both need your eyes checked."

He could feel her heart beating rapidly against his chest.

"Luc said you used to watch me ten years ago. Be careful you don't get a crush on me again." He tried to tease a smile out of her.

"Don't what?" Her voice was immediately defensive.

Way to go, Morgan. You've really gotten off on the wrong foot now. He had meant it as a joke. He'd expected her to laugh. How was he going to talk himself out of this one? "Get a crush on me again."

He laughed, hoping she would pick up on the joke. "On second thought, go ahead. It's okay. I like the idea."

"You might like the *idea*, Morgan. But I'm not fourteen years old anymore, in case you haven't noticed."

His eyes ran over her face, then looked down to where her breasts lay against his chest, rising and falling with each angry breath she took. "I've noticed," he assured her.

She ignored his perusal. "Then we both agree I'm well beyond the age of crushes."

"Well . . . maybe not a crush then. But there's definitely something going on between us."

"In your imagination."

In defense of his point, he could point out the physical responses she was having to his nearness, but he didn't want to argue with her. He had her in his arms—he wanted to savor the moment, revel in the physical response he was having to her and antic-ipate the joys awaiting them.

At the end of the song, Morgan walked her back to the table. She was grateful the ordeal was over. She loved the feel of his arms holding her, but his blunt acknowledgment that she'd been watching him and his accusation of a developing crush had made her angry.

Who did he think he was treating her like a love-struck teenager? Even his straight forward rejection of her had been easier to accept.

Obviously his concern for her feelings earlier this

evening had just been part of his good host role. She couldn't wait until this whole disastrous weekend was over!

"Why don't you and Carol join Luc and me at our table?"

Oh, sure, and let him play Mr. Teenager's Heartthrob for the rest of the evening? Fat chance! "No, thank you. We're ready to call it a night." She looked at Carol, hoping for confirmation.

"Yes, we had a long day of sightseeing and I'm really tired." With insight from long years of friendship, Carol backed her up.

"Let me walk you to your car then."

"That's not necessary."

"I'm just trying to look out for your best interests."

"Don't! I already have *one* big brother, Morgan. I don't need two."

Morgan looked as if he wanted to say more, but instead he turned and went back to his table.

"Are you really ready to leave?" Melissa asked Carol.

"I was ready half an hour ago, but I was hoping the two of you would quit playing games with each other and get something going. You were a little hard on him, don't you think? What did he say to you while you were dancing? You had a real funny look on your face."

"Why don't we discuss this in the car?" It was hard to force herself not to have one last look across the room, but Melissa succeeded. She gathered her purse and headed for the exit.

*　　*　　*

It was pointless to toss and turn, so she turned on her bedside light and tried to read. That didn't work, either.

When she was little her mother had always made her warm milk with honey when she couldn't get to sleep. Something within her longed for the remembered comfort.

She didn't think Evelyn would mind if she indulged herself, as long as she was quiet. She put her robe on over her nightgown and headed for the kitchen.

She was sitting at the kitchen table drinking her warm milk with honey when she heard the door swing open. Turning, she saw Morgan standing in the doorway. He looked surprised to see her.

Her first thought was to take her drink and head back to her room, but then she remembered what Carol had said on the drive home. Carol thought the two of them needed to sit down and talk civilly about what was or was not going on between them. Get all the cards out on the table and then go from there.

Maybe this was their chance to do just that.

"Trouble sleeping?" he asked.

"A little," she admitted.

He walked over to the table. A pair of white sweatpants, riding low on his hips, was all he had on. Melissa let her eyes roam over the glorious expanse of his tanned chest. Broad shoulders, well muscled arms—she'd never be able to look at him fully clothed again without thinking of the flawless body underneath.

Morgan picked up her mug and took a sip. "Warm

milk?'' He leaned over her back and placed the mug in front of her again. Still bent over her, he whispered in her ear, "A cold shower is a better cure for what's bothering you, angel."

He trailed his fingers along the back of her neck before standing up, walking around to the other side of the table and sitting down across from her.

So much for talking civilly. Oh, how she would love to wipe that smug smile off his face. "Since I haven't had my cold shower, it's awfully brave of you to be in the same room with me, half undressed as you are. Aren't you afraid I'll attack you?"

"I didn't know you were here."

"Well . . . now that you do, you could go back to your room and finish dressing." She took a sip of her milk, trying valiantly to hold back her body's physical reaction to him. It didn't seem to care that she was angry at Morgan, all it knew was that he was nearby and it was going into sensory overload.

"Why? It doesn't bother you, does it?" He leaned back in his chair, folding his arms over his chest.

Melissa shrugged.

"This is more than I wear to the beach," Morgan persisted.

It was true, but at least at the beach there would be other people around. Although she doubted whether her traitorous body would make any concessions for a crowd. "This isn't the beach, Morgan."

Morgan held his hands up in a gesture of defeat. "All right, I'll go put on a shirt. But you'd think a twenty-four-year-old who's grown up in southern

California would be used to the sight of men without shirts.''

Men without shirts didn't bother her. Just *this* man without his shirt! But there was no way she was going to let him know that. "You're right. I've seen plenty of men at the beach. Plus I have an older brother . . . and an ex-fiancé.''

"Ex-fiancé . . . that's right. I almost forgot you *are* on the rebound, aren't you? I'll go get my shirt.'' He started to get up.

Melissa stood up slowly, scowling down at him. "Don't you dare.'' First he'd made her sound like a prudish school marm, now he made it sound as though he feared she might attack him after all. It was a real struggle not to pick up her milk and pour it over his head.

"Will you calm down, Melly, I'm just teasing you.''

"Teasing?'' She raised one eyebrow.

"Yes. Just like I was teasing you while we were dancing.''

"About the crush?''

"Yes.''

"And the cold shower?''

"Well . . .'' One side of his mouth turned up in an amused half smile.

"You're hedging.''

"Wishful thinking, maybe?''

"Are you or aren't you accusing me of having a case of lust?''

"Not exactly, but don't try to tell me you're completely indifferent to me. I can take you in my arms and prove differently.''

Oh, how part of her wished he would. But the other part was still angered by his arrogance and not completely convinced he had been teasing. ''It never occurred to you that I might be in love with you?'' *Good heavens, where had that come from?*

He snapped to attention, his eyes narrowing. ''Do you think you're in love with me?''

''Hardly.'' Placing both hands on the table, she leaned toward him. ''I don't even think I like you.'' Straightening up, she stormed out of the room.

He was making a mess of this! He was trying to woo her with his teasing charm, but everything he said seemed to blow up in his face. He was expecting her to laugh and she was becoming more and more defensive.

Nothing like this had ever happened to him. Sure he'd had trouble with women—trouble getting rid of them.

He couldn't blame her for being angry with him. Twice she'd made reference to the two of them forming a relationship. Both times he'd rejected the idea. He couldn't expect her to suggest it again.

He didn't blame her for throwing Marshall back at him, either, although it was ego bruising. Marshall would be in good shape, of course, since he was a professional athlete in his prime. The thought of all that prime focused on Melly made him want to put his fist through something.

His hopes had soared when she'd asked if he'd

considered the possibility that she was in love with him. He wasn't quite so optimistic, but he hadn't considered that she might not like him at all.

He suspected her parting shot had been fired in anger and wasn't completely accurate. At least he *hoped* she hadn't meant it. It seemed to him there was more than anger flashing in her eyes though.

It was clear he was going to have to start over. A complete retreat and regrouping before he tried again.

Melissa put off leaving her room as long as possible the next morning. But her efforts were wasted. Carol showed up with the news that Morgan and Luc had already left to go back to San Diego.

She was grateful she wouldn't have to face him again. She couldn't believe she'd almost told him she loved him. Heck, she was having trouble accepting that she did. Awareness of her love for him had slammed into her as she'd questioned him about the possibility.

At breakfast, no one mentioned Morgan and Lucas's early departure. Melissa was going through the motions, willing the hours to go by so she and Carol could also leave.

Finally the time came to pack. Melissa went gratefully to her room alone.

She knew from the looks Carol was giving her that she suspected something was up, although she hadn't asked. For the first time since this roller-coaster ride with Morgan began, she didn't feel like discussing him with her best friend.

She had acknowledged her love for Morgan to herself, but somehow she couldn't bring herself to say the words out loud, not even to Carol.

While she was packing, Evelyn came to the door. "Can we talk for a minute, Melissa?"

"Sure, come on in."

Evelyn closed the door behind herself and took a seat on the edge of the bed.

"When Morgan first called to tell us he had been in touch with you all again, I was surprised how much more he talked about you than Lucas. After all they were best friends. The next time he called he mentioned your engagement and the house he was designing. Next thing I know he's calling and asking if I'd like company for the weekend."

Melissa sat down next to Evelyn, unable to believe what she was hearing. "This weekend was Morgan's idea?"

"Yes, it was. And I don't think things went quite the way he'd planned or he wouldn't have left so early this morning."

"I guess not." Melissa thought back over their argument in the kitchen.

"I know it's all none of my business, but if the problem was caused by what Mitch said last night, I hope you'll reconsider. Mitch was way out of line and you have a right to be angry at him, but don't let him influence your relationship with Morgan." She reached over and gave Melissa's hand a pat.

"Anyway, I've said more than I intended to . . . I'll leave now so you can finish packing."

No, Mitch hadn't created the problems between her and Morgan. In fact, the moments they'd shared after his wild proposition had been the best moments they'd shared all weekend.

She couldn't get over it . . . This weekend had been Morgan's idea. She wondered what he had originally planned for this weekend. She had no idea, but she had an awful feeling that somehow she'd been part of the reason things hadn't gone right.

Now where did they go from here?

NINE

The flowers were delivered at one o'clock . . . and two o'clock . . . and three o'clock . . . and four o'clock.

So when there was another knock on her office door at five o'clock, Melissa wasn't surprised.

She was putting files away in the filing cabinet, her back to the door. "Just set them in the middle of the desk. It's the only spot left and I'm getting ready to go home for the day anyway."

"Care to take a short detour for dinner first?"

Melissa recognized the voice . . . and it wasn't the delivery man from Ye Olde Flower Shoppe!

She closed the cabinet drawer and turned around slowly. He was standing in the front of her desk, looking over the assorted floral arrangements placed around the outer edges of her work space.

"Nice flowers. Looks like some guy's trying to apologize for being a real Neanderthal."

She walked over to stand behind her desk. "I don't know. None of them came with a card." She looked him straight in the eye, trying to ignore his little-boy grin—a grin that admitted to mischief, but asked for a treat anyway. She'd seen Brian that morning to get Luc's cards and had thought the flowers might be from him. She had hoped they were from Morgan.

Looking down, he reached out to run one long, tanned finger down the side of a red rosebud. "Being an expert on Neanderthal traditions, I would say you could count on the sender showing up with an invitation to dinner."

She fought to contain the smile that threatened. "And in your expert opinion, what should my response be to this invitation?"

"That depends." He stopped his examination of the rose and turned the full force of his blue gaze on her. The little boy was gone, leaving behind a man unsure of his reception. "If you're willing to overlook his past mistakes and give him a chance to start over, you should accept the invitation. But if you'd rather he took a flying leap, you could tell him where to put his invitation and his flowers."

He hadn't offered any explanations for why he had rejected her initially or why he'd had a change of heart. But he was here trying to make amends and their arguments at his parents' house hadn't been all his fault. "What if I've made some mistakes, too, maybe said some things I didn't really mean?" She caught her bottom lip between her teeth.

"He's obviously willing to overlook it, or he wouldn't have sent the flowers."

"I'm sorry, Morgan."

"Me, too. Dinner?"

"I'd love to."

They ran into Lucas in the parking lot. Melissa told him she'd left his Trivial Pursuit cards on his desk.

"Thanks, I appreciate it. By the way, the El Cajon store is out of monthly sales flyers."

"There are some extras in my filing cabinet. I'll go get them for you."

He held up his hand. "No . . . no, there's no hurry. I won't be heading out that way again until tomorrow. You can get them to me in the morning. Have a nice evening." With an I-told-you-so smile for Morgan and a wink for Melissa, he headed into the building.

Morgan continued walking her to her car. "So, you saw Marshall today?"

"Yes, this morning."

He nodded thoughtfully. "Any problems."

"Problems?" *What was he getting at?*

"Did he try anything?"

Understanding came to her. "You want to know if he came on to me this morning."

"I was wondering if there were any signs of a reconciliation in sight. I guess the answer to both questions would be the same."

"You're right. The answer to both questions is

no." She looked up at him. "You were worried about me seeing Brian, weren't you?"

"No . . ." He started to deny it. Then he shrugged his shoulders and admitted, "Yes, I was worried."

She wondered at the confusing array of emotions that had flickered in his eyes. "Don't be." She reached up to run her hand down the side of his face.

He started to lean toward her. When a passing car honked at them, he straightened. "Guess we'd better get going."

They went to Melissa's apartment first, to drop off her car. She also took a quick shower and changed out of her work clothes and into a softly flowing red dress that buttoned up the front.

She knew Morgan liked her choice by the gleam in his eye when she walked into the living room. "Ready?" he asked.

"Yes." She had been ready and waiting for this evening for years.

It was a short ride to the elegant beachside restaurant. A sense of wonder and excitement surrounded Melissa. This wasn't just another dinner date . . . this one was with Morgan.

Her body was having its usual reaction to his nearness, but armed with the knowledge of her newfound love, she didn't try to stop it.

Melissa had been to the Lobster Quadrille several times for lunch and was amazed at how different it looked at night. The normally bright, sunny dining room was now in an intimate semidarkness.

The staff was efficient but nonintrusive, each course seeming to appear and disappear right on cue. When Melissa's knife slipped off the edge of her plate onto the table, it was immediately whisked away and replaced with a new one.

Everything about the evening was perfect: the atmosphere, the food, the service, and especially the company.

They talked about Morgan's plans for expanding his business and Melissa's plans for starting her own. Their eyes met and held often, their surroundings and the other diners fading away into nonexistence. A pulsing shock of awareness sparked between them with each accidental touch of their hands.

Melissa was too full for dessert, but she lingered over coffee, not wanting the evening to end. She tucked every second away in her memory.

As they were getting ready to leave, their waiter presented Melissa with a red rose.

"Think you need another flower?" Morgan winked at her.

"A few more and I'll be ready to open my own shop."

Morgan took her arm and headed out of the dining room. "Feel up to a stroll on the beach?" he asked.

"All right."

The front door opened and a couple entered.

"Lissa, what a surprise!" Beverly Marshall's voice stopped Melissa in her tracks. Beverly introduced her to her date, then looked up to the man standing behind Melissa.

"Morgan?" Beverly looked puzzled, then smiled

brightly. "Well, of course, you are an *old* family friend, aren't you?" Her inflection made it clear she was referring to more than the amount of time Morgan had know the Ellisons.

Morgan acknowledged Beverly's greeting stiffly.

"Isn't it nice of you to try to cheer up our Lissa." She reached over and patted Melissa's arm. "I'm just so exasperated with Brian, let me tell you. I don't know what to do with that boy."

"Bev, our table's ready." Beverly's date broke into her monologue.

"Coming. I'll give Brian your regards, Lissa. Although I don't think I'll mention seeing you with Morgan. Unless . . ." Beverly's eyes lit up and Melissa knew she was working on some kind of plan. "Well, good night, you two."

"Enjoy your dinner, Beverly."

"Thank you, Morgan. I'm sure I will." The couple followed the maître d' into the dining room.

"Still feel like walking?" Morgan asked Melissa.

"Yes." The thought of fresh air appealed to her more than ever.

She pushed all thoughts of Beverly and Brian out of her mind as they exited the restaurant on the beach side, walking down a flight of stairs to the sand below. This was *her* night with Morgan and she wasn't going to let anyone or anything intrude on it.

Morgan took her rose and put it in his jacket pocket. He took her hand in his, setting off yet another wave of awareness racing through her.

The sand shifted beneath their feet as they walked

toward the shoreline. A cool breeze blew the salty scent of the sea to them.

They stopped just above the tidemark to watch the waves. The moonlight cast a sparkling trail across the undulating water.

Morgan stood behind her, wrapping his arms around her waist to pull her back against him. The heat of his body scorched through their clothing to warm her skin underneath.

Leaning her head back onto his chest, she felt him gently kiss the top of her head—or it might only have been the wind ruffling her hair.

After several minutes, Morgan unwrapped his arms to take hold of her shoulders and turn her toward him. Her lips parted slightly as she looked up at him expectantly. She knew he was going to kiss her and she went up on her toes to meet him halfway.

Morgan moved his mouth toward hers, stopping only inches from her lips. "Sweet Melly," he whispered, his eyes glinting with sparks of captured moonlight.

"Morgan." His name was part of the kiss, as once again she experienced the warmth of his lips on hers.

The effect it had on her bewildered body was as devastating as it had been the first time. She reached up to wrap her arms around his neck as a drowning person reaches for a lifeline.

Unlike the kiss in his car, where space was limited, all of her could now reach all of him. The combined sensations of his body pressed against hers and their mouths rediscovering each other sent shivers racing through her.

"You're cold." Morgan removed his suit jacket and draped it over her shoulders. She snuggled down into it, absorbing his warmth and inhaling the scent of his aftershave.

He ran his hands beneath the lapels of his jacket as he held it around her. "I can't believe I almost let this chance slip away from us." He kissed her again—a kiss filled with promises of new beginnings.

Melissa's hands were between them, pressing tightly against his chest, feeling the strong, rhythmic beat of his heart and the expanding of his chest with each short, shallow breath he took.

A wave of yearning crashed over her, her knees threatening to give out. She leaned into him, resting more of her weight on his hard, muscled length. His hands let go of the jacket and moved back around her, pulling her more tightly against him.

Lifting his head, he looked down at her. "I don't understand what you do to me with your magic kisses." He reached up and smoothed her hair.

Morgan had felt the magic between them. It wasn't all her imagination! "I was wondering the same thing."

"Then you *do* feel it, too?"

"Oh, yes . . ." She placed a kiss on his chin.

"What's next for us, Melly?"

"I was hoping you might have some suggestions."

"Would you think I was rushing things if I suggested my apartment?"

"Under normal circumstances, I'd have to say yes."

"Are these normal circumstances?"

"No. No they aren't." There was definitely nothing normal about the circumstances they were in. All they had been through in the past and the confusion of the last few weeks.

She knew her acceptance of the invitation to his apartment was an agreement to go to bed with him. Surprisingly, she wasn't as nervous as she'd imagined she would be.

He leaned down and gave her one last kiss before heading back to the restaurant, his arm around her shoulder, as he held her closely against his side.

He hoped he wasn't moving too fast. He had originally planned to take her back to her apartment after dinner and leave her at the door with a good-night kiss and arrangements for dinner and a movie the next night.

But his plans had fallen apart the second he'd kissed her.

He'd managed to convince himself that his memory had exaggerated the intense response his body had experienced when he'd kissed her before, but it hadn't. If anything it had underplayed it.

When she'd moved tightly against him, it had taken every ounce of his willpower not to pull her down to the sand and make love to her then and there. When was the last time a woman's kiss had filled him with such urgency?

Could part of it be Beverly Marshall's remarks?

He hadn't missed her implications about the age difference between him and Melly. And he hadn't missed her optimism that Melly and her son would be getting back together. Was this urgency he felt linked to some primal need to bond Melly to him quickly in case Marshall did change his mind or a desperate attempt to be with her as much as he could, while he could?

Although he hadn't planned on the two of them making love tonight, he had expected they would in the near future. So luckily, the proper protection was ready and waiting at his apartment.

Neither of them had said much since they'd gotten into the car. He wondered what she was thinking.

He stopped the car at a red light. A right turn would take him to Melly's apartment—his lay straight ahead. "I could still take you home if you'd like," he offered. It would kill him to take her home, but he wanted to be sure she had no regrets.

"No. I want to go with you."

He turned and looked at her. She smiled up at him, her eyes filled with desire and trust.

The trust bothered him. Not that he would ever deliberately do anything to hurt her—the last thing he wanted to do was hurt her. But he couldn't return her trust.

He would have to make it up to her in other ways. . . .

TEN

Morgan was subletting the apartment he was living in, so the furnishing and decor had all been chosen by someone else. While Melissa didn't think its stark modernness quite seemed to suit him, it was comfortable.

He had put some soft jazz on the stereo and built a fire in the fireplace. Melissa sat on the white leather couch, curled up next to him—listening to the music, watching the fire and the shadows it made.

She involuntarily slid into a daydream, reliving the feeling of being in his arms, with his lips on hers and his hands gently caressing her. Once again she felt herself shiver.

"Are you *still* cold?" Morgan rose to put another log on the fire. "Come over here, it's warmer." Stretching out on the rug in front of the fireplace, he lay on his side, propping himself up on an elbow.

Melissa got up slowly. The flames crackling in the fireplace and the flames of desire burning in Morgan's eyes drew her to them.

He reached his hand up and gently pulled her down beside him. She lay on her side facing him, watching the flickering light from the fire play across his features. It looked like his lips whispered something, but she couldn't be sure, it might have been an illusion of the firelight.

With one unhurried motion he pulled her closer to him and turned her shoulders to the floor, cradling her neck on his arm.

Melissa's heart pounded an uneven rhythm. She was surprised by the strength of the passion on Morgan's face and the yearning she felt in response to it. He began moving his mouth toward hers, but the few moments of waiting seemed like hours to Melissa.

His kiss was gentle and teasing, the complete opposite of what his eyes had promised and certainly not what she needed to satisfy the gnawing hunger seeping through her body. A frustrated moan escaped her and she reached her arms up around the back of his neck to pull him closer.

Her simple movement seemed to unleash the hold Morgan had been keeping on his desire—his kiss growing hard and demanding. Melissa had no trouble meeting the demands.

She was breathless as Morgan moved his lips from hers and slowly ran his mouth along her jaw and down her neck to burrow just above her collarbone.

The path he took burned from the heat of his kisses and his ragged breath.

He continued the journey downward, moving along the edge of her neckline. His fingers made quick work of her top buttons. He parted her dress, nudging it over inch by inch, until she felt cool air sweep over her exposed skin.

The front clasp of her bra surrendered to him just as easily as her buttons had. His warm hands gently molded around her bare breasts, causing a tingly ache that was followed by an overwhelming burst of sensations as he covered the aroused peak with his warm, moist mouth—alternately teasing with his tongue and nipping gently with his teeth.

Melissa was unable to fight the tides that were rushing over her. She lay luxuriating in them until she found her hands aching to touch him in return.

Slowly unwinding her fingers from his hair, she let them run over the taut, hard muscles along the back of his neck. Unbelievably, the muscles tightened even more as her fingers played over them.

She moved her hands outward across the vast width of his shoulders, then inward to the center of his back to travel down. She loved the hard feel of him and the ripples that ran through his muscles.

When her hands worked their way even lower, Morgan moved in response to her touch—his hips pushing forward against her. The sound that rose up from the depths of her chest was part moan, part sigh, and part whimper.

Morgan lifted his head. "Everything all right?"

She opened her eyes to meet his gaze. "Never better," she assured him.

He lowered his head again to place a final kiss on her breast and then retraced the path back to her lips. He kissed her deeply, his tongue stroking the sensitive roof of her mouth and the inside of her lips.

Once again he moved his mouth off hers, this time to repeat his sweet torments along her other side.

The tremor that now rippled through her body worked its way from the inside out.

"Still cold? Maybe this will help." Morgan moved his body until it covered hers. At first the smooth material of his shirt felt cool against her naked breasts, but then she could feel the heat radiating from the man beneath.

She slipped her hands between them, untied his tie, opened his buttons, then pushed his shirt aside until flesh met flesh. The crisp, curling hairs on his chest felt rough against her satiny skin.

Then he was kissing her again and she felt her body arching up to mold its soft curves to his hardness.

"Warm now?" He smiled down at her.

Her affirmative answer was a contented purr.

"More than warm?" he teased.

Breathless, her voice came out in a husky whisper, "I have dreamed and fantasized about this moment so many times. I imagined how you would feel and how it would feel for you to touch me. I'd pictured candlelight instead of the fireplace and satin robes instead of clothes, glasses of champagne . . ." Her voice trailed off. She moved against him, her hands pulling him close.

But Morgan was retreating from her. She could see it in his eyes moments before he lifted his body off hers. What had she done wrong?

"Melly." There was a wistful quality to his voice, "I'm not just yesterday's fantasy. I'm a flesh-and-blood man."

"I know that." How could he doubt that she did?

He shook his head. "Do you?"

"Of course."

He looked deep into her love-soft eyes. "I'm not sure you do."

He started reaching for her and her heart soared. But it plummeted back to earth as he hooked her bra and buttoned her dress, his touch proficient and clinical. "I could compete with another man, Melly, but I can't compete with a fantasy vision of perfection."

"You wouldn't be." She reached out for him, but he stood up and moved away from her.

"Wouldn't I?" He ran his hands through his hair. "Melly, this isn't a game for me. I want you because of who you are and how you make me feel, not because you fit the part of some romantic vision in my mind."

"That's not why I want you, either," she protested, but he didn't seem to be listening.

She sat up on the white rug, her red dress fanning out around her. She hadn't said what she'd said to make Morgan think he had to compete with her fantasies—she'd been looking for some way to let him know how wonderful he was making her feel. Unfortunately, he didn't seem to understand and she wasn't sure she could explain without digging herself in deeper.

Silently, she watched him button his shirt, tie his tie, and put on his jacket that he had draped over the arm of the couch. She stared at the rosebud, just visible at the top of his pocket.

Following her gaze to the flower, he reached down and removed it. He walked over to where she was sitting, held the rose out to her with one hand, and offered the other to help her up.

The ride back to her apartment was also made in silence. It was only when they reached her door and she had unlocked it that she spoke. "Guess I should thank you. It was nice while it lasted." She turned from him and started in the door.

He took hold of her shoulders and pulled her back around to face him.

"It's not over, Melly. I just think we need to slow down. This was just our first date," he reminded her.

"And you've never slept with someone on the first date before?"

"I have," he confessed. "Have you?"

"No." *Not the first, the second, the third* . . . the longing, the desire had never been there until now.

"All the more reason we shouldn't jump into anything."

Maybe he had a point, she was willing to grant him that much. But she still felt like she had when she'd taken her favorite stuffed rabbit for show and tell only to find that Cuddles had slipped out a hole in the bottom of her bookbag somewhere between school and home. It was an empty lost feeling. An if-I'd-only-been-more-careful feeling.

"Good night, Melly. I'll call you." He kissed her lips gently before leaving her.

Melissa entered the apartment. Luckily, Carol appeared to have already gone to bed for the evening. She put her rose into a bud vase, placed it on her nightstand, changed into a nightgown, turned off the light, and climbed into bed.

She couldn't help wondering about the bed she had almost spent the night in. What color was the bedspread . . . the sheets. What size was it? What difference did it make? She doubted she'd get a second chance to find out.

He hadn't slammed the door in her face completely, he said he'd call . . . but how many times had she heard that in the past? He'd said they would take things more slowly, but had he said that just to pacify her. Was it really over?

She ran back over the evening in her mind, from the moment he'd arrived in her office to the moment he'd left her at her door. She wouldn't change any of it, except the ending.

Maybe she should have told him she loved him. Would there have been a difference in his reaction?

She knew the difference between fantasy and reality, especially when it came to Morgan. The reality was much better than the fantasy. What was the harm in comparing the two?

*   *   *

When he got back to his apartment, Morgan stretched out on the rug in front of the fireplace. The loneliness of the king-size bed in the next room didn't appeal to him. He wanted to be here, where a short time ago he'd held Melly in his arms.

He thought back to the night they'd danced at the Desert Chic. Had he accidentally stumbled on the truth when he was trying to lighten her mood? Did she have a crush on him?

She'd strongly denied the possibility of it. Was her denial just a cover? She'd said she was too old for crushes. Was there an age limit on crushes?

When he'd looked in her eyes, he couldn't tell if she was seeing him or living a piece of a past fantasy, surrendering to a Prince Charming she'd built up in her mind, using him as the foundation.

He wanted her to want him for who he was, not for who she imagined him to be. Had they spent enough time together for her to know him?

He'd criticized her for getting engaged to Marshall after only three months and here he was rushing her off to bed less than one month after meeting her again. But he felt like he'd known her forever.

They'd also mentioned the possibility of it being a case of lust. Could that be? If it was a simple case of hormones, how would taking her to bed affect their relationship? Would she tuck the experience away with the rest of her fantasies and move on or would she stay with him?

She'll stay if you can do it better than you did in her dreams.

He was good, or so he'd been told. Wasn't it bad enough that he had to follow the Mighty Marshall . . . now he was expected to take on the ultimate fantasy lover?

And why did measuring up matter so much to him? A woman's satisfaction had always been important, but he'd never been so obsessively worried about having to be a woman's best lover. Why did it matter with Melly?

He didn't know why . . . he just knew it mattered. He *had* to be better than Marshall, better than any other lover she'd had and better than her best fantasy.

ELEVEN

Marshall House was well underway, far enough along that Marshall's agent had called Morgan and asked him to come out to the site for some publicity shots and an interview with Brian for the Home section of the paper.

He felt a bit smug as he approached the site, remembering the morning he'd made the trip and found Melly with Marshall. Now she was his. . . .

For the past few weeks they'd been dating. He'd been very careful to avoid situations where they might get carried away physically, but they were spending a lot of time together getting to know each other—although most of the time he felt he'd known her forever, he wanted her to feel the same way about him. He wanted her to know him as he really was, not how she'd fantasized him.

Brian was already there when Morgan arrived. The reporter and photographer got there shortly afterward.

It was a pretty routine interview from his end. He discussed how he tried to balance the aesthetics of the project with the functional needs of the future inhabitants and conservation considerations.

The reporter turned his attention to Brian. Morgan was only half listening, until he heard the man ask, "Did you make many changes in the house after your engagement was canceled?"

"No. I saw no reason to."

"Have you seen Melissa lately?"

"We had lunch together today."

Morgan looked at Brian, his eyes narrowing. Melly had had lunch with Marshall today? It was news to him. Morgan wondered if Marshall knew about the two of them? Had his mother told him— had Melly?

"Any chance of a reconciliation?" the reporter continued.

Brian smiled noncommittally. "I'd rather not comment on that." He slid his left hand casually into his pants pocket. "Any other questions about the house?"

Don't overreact. There's probably an innocent explanation, pal, Morgan reminded himself as he headed for the sporting goods store to talk to Melly.

His uneasiness increased and his temper kicked in when he found out that she had left work shortly after returning from lunch.

This isn't Emmie, man, this is Melly. Don't go overboard until you have the whole story. But that was easier said than done. The quote "History repeats itself'' kept running through his mind despite his attempts to banish it.

He and Melly weren't scheduled to see each other until tomorrow night, but he needed to see her now. He was supposed to be having his usual Tuesday night racquetball game with Luc this evening.

Since Luc wasn't at the store, either, he used his cellular phone to leave a message on Luc's answering machine to cancel their game, and headed for Melly's apartment.

The doorbell rang just as Melissa was putting the finishing touches on the table setting. She had invited her father to dinner. Her mother was having a church committee meeting at the house and rather than have Frank banished to the den, Melissa had offered to fix him dinner at her apartment.

"Just a minute," she called. "You're early," she said, opening the door. Instead of her father, she saw Morgan.

She started to smile at the unexpected pleasure, but the expression on his face stopped her. His mouth was a thin line, his eyes looked cold, and the square lines of his jaw were tightened in anger.

"You were expecting someone else." It was more statement than question. "I won't stay long," he continued as he walked in.

Melissa wondered what he was doing here and why he looked so angry. It was Tuesday, he was supposed to be playing racquetball with Lucas.

"So, can I get you something to drink?" *Great,*

Melissa, when in doubt, haul out the good-hostess routine.

"A glass of ice water would be nice."

He followed her into the kitchen. As she fixed his water, he wandered around the room.

"Let's see—new bottle of Scotch, something that smells delicious cooking in the oven, a very attractive dress . . ." His eyes ran over her, lingering on her feminine curves. She had no control over the rush of heat fluttering through her at his frank appraisal.

She handed him his water. He acknowledged it with a nod and headed for the dining room. *What was with him?*

"Candles on the table for two, flowers, wine . . ." He picked up the bottle and read the label. "Nice choice." He set the bottle back down, took a sip of his water, and then turned to face Melissa. "It doesn't take Sherlock Holmes to deduce that you're expecting a man for dinner . . . a very special man."

Melissa didn't like the tone of his voice or his attitude, disliked it enough that instead of telling him her father was coming to dinner, she said, "Right on the money, Morgan."

"Who's coming to dinner, Melly? Brian? The sportswear salesman who was drooling over you the other day?"

"How do you know about the sportswear salesman?"

"Lucas."

Now why didn't that surprise her? "Are you paying him to spy on me or is he doing it as a favor for an old friend?" she asked angrily.

Darn Lucas, why couldn't he keep his nose out of her business? She wondered if Luc had arranged Morgan's sudden appearance at her door. She was unhappy with Luc's continued interference, but what bothered her most was Morgan's angry accusations that she was seeing someone else.

"He's not spying. I had a racquetball game with him the day the salesman had been in, and he just happened to mention it."

"Like he just happened to mention I was having company for dinner tonight?"

"No, I haven't talked to Luc today. Have you?"

"I talked to him this morning. We're organizing the Christmas sales."

"Talk to anyone else interesting today?" His eyes shot fire at her.

Suddenly she knew—Brian, this had to do with Brian. Somehow he knew she'd seen Brian today. "I talked to quite a few people today in a business capacity. Anyone in particular you're interested in?"

"Don't play games with me."

"I'm not." She squared her shoulders. "If you have something specific to ask me, ask."

"Did you see Marshall today?"

"Yes."

"At least you don't deny it."

"Why should I deny it? I have nothing to hide."

She wouldn't have believed it was possible, but he looked even angrier now than when he'd arrived. "I know we agreed to slow down the pace of our relationship, but I did expect there would be fidelity."

"First off, *we* never *agreed* to slow down the

pace. *You decided.* And secondly, I assumed fidelity was part of the arrangement, too.''

"You call lunching with Marshall and having him to your apartment for dinner fidelity?"

"Brian came into the store to drop off an autographed baseball and some pictures for a sales promotion we've got coming up."

"He could have had a courier deliver them."

"He could have, but he didn't. He made that decision. I didn't ask him to deliver them personally! Since it was around lunchtime, he asked me to lunch, and since he is still a friend, I accepted. But it was *not* a date, Morgan."

"You might not see it that way, but Marshall does."

"I don't think so. You seem to have forgotten, he's the one who called off our wedding."

"Melly, don't be so naive. I was standing right next to him when he told a reporter that the two of you had had lunch together. Then when the man asked if there was a reconciliation in the making, he didn't deny it."

"I have no control over what he decides to tell the press. But I guarantee you it was just a simple lunch between friends."

"Then what's all this?" he gestured to the table. "Who's coming to dinner?" he asked as coolly as if he'd been inquiring what was on the menu.

"Morgan, I don't like your accusations." Her anger intensified. "You honestly believe I would go out with you on Monday, see some mystery man on

Tuesday, and then go out with you again on Wednesday?''

He set his glass down on the table and walked over to stand several inches away from her. His feet were aggressively planted at shoulder width.

With one finger, he tilted her chin up until he was looking her straight in the eye. Melissa felt her body moving involuntarily toward his, as if it were being drawn by a magnet. ''Who's coming to dinner, Melly?'' he whispered.

Melissa pulled back sharply. ''I told you I feel strongly about fidelity in our relationship. You shouldn't suspect that I would be spending time alone with anyone you would have objections to.''

''I need to know.'' He ignored her statements.

''Why?''

''If you weren't trying to hide something from me, you would have told me right up front who was coming.''

''If you'd asked nicely, maybe. But you came barging in here, your mind made up that I was seeing someone else. Don't you think you were a bit unfair?''

He didn't answer her. Going back to the table, he retrieved his glass, went over to the couch, and sat down. He placed his glass on the end table before leaning back with his hands behind his head.

''What do you think you're doing?''

''It's obvious you're not going to tell me who your dinner guest is. I'll just have to wait until he gets here and see for myself.''

She would love to let him stay, love to see the

look on his face when her father walked in. On the other hand, she didn't want him to think he could get away with this arrogant, domineering attitude.

"Of all the nerve," Melissa fumed. "I think you'd better leave now."

When Morgan didn't move, she walked over and grabbed his arm in an attempt to pull him up. She didn't think for an instant she could actually budge him, but she felt she had to make some show of resistance, no matter how futile.

Morgan brought his leg up, knocking her off balance, and caught her in his arms. He looked down at her, the haunted look in his blue eyes, silencing any protest she might have made.

The kiss started softly, but it soon became deeper and more demanding. Her anger dissolved. The past few weeks all he had given her were chaste goodnight kisses. She had missed this closeness with him and the wild magic he could stir in her.

The hand that grasped his arm loosened its grip and slid upward to caress the back of his neck, while the other moved slowly across the front of his chest.

Morgan kept one arm tightly around her waist, as if he thought she might try to get away—although her every movement denied the possibility. His other hand moved teasingly within the edges of the V-shaped neckline of her dress.

A familiar sound was trying to fight through the haze in her mind.

"Melly, the doorbell," Morgan whispered against her lips.

The doorbell!

Morgan released her, Melissa got to her feet and instinctively started to straighten her dress and hair.

"You can fix your dress and hair, but you can't erase the glow on your cheeks or the fire burning in your eyes. Any fool can see you've just been kissed, and kissed well."

His remarks refueled her anger. How could he still think she was seeing someone else after all she'd said and with the way she responded so strongly to him physically?

Melissa bit her tongue and headed for the door. She reached it just as the bell rang again. "We'll see who gets the last laugh, Morgan Edwards," she said under her breath.

She opened the door to let her father in. "Hi, Daddy." She gave him a hug and kiss.

"How's my girl? Dinner smells great. I'm starving."

Closing the door and turning back to face the living room, Melissa caught only a brief look of shock on Morgan's face before he gained his composure and rose to shake the older man's hand.

Frank looked as surprised to see Morgan as Morgan was to see him, but his greeting was friendly. He did a double-take at Melissa's face and Morgan's hair but didn't say anything.

"Well, I'll be going, so you can get to your dinner."

"You're not joining us?" Frank asked.

"Would you like to stay? There's plenty," Melissa invited, her mouth smiling innocently while her eyes sent I-told-you-so messages.

"If you're sure it wouldn't be an imposition?"

"Guess I'll wash up." Frank headed for the bathroom.

Morgan looked down at her angrily. "Stop looking so pleased with yourself."

"My, aren't we touchy?"

"Why didn't you just tell me it was your father you were expecting?"

"You should have trusted me."

"Like Brian trusted you the afternoon we were kissing in my car?"

Melissa felt the blood drain from her face as desolation tore at her heart. "I didn't plan that."

"God, Melly, I didn't mean it." He started to reach for her, but Frank returned.

Melissa put on a smile for her father's benefit. "Why don't you wash up, too, Morgan. I'll get dinner on the table."

She didn't know why he was bothering to stay. His opinion of her seemed pretty set and not at all flattering.

Her father followed her into the kitchen. It was a real struggle to push her emotional turmoil to the back of her mind and act normally.

"So . . . Morgan wasn't originally invited to dinner?"

"No, he just happened to stop by." She put the food into the serving bowls. Frank helped her carry them into the dining room.

"You two *seeing* each other?"

"We have been." *Whether they still were remained to be seen*.

"Getting serious?"

"We've only been going out for a couple of weeks." She set a third place at the table.

"When I first saw Morgan here, I thought maybe he was here to ask me for your hand."

"Don't hold your breath, Daddy."

He couldn't believe he'd said that to her! He knew the kiss in his car had been unplanned . . . spontaneous. She hadn't planned it any more than he had.

His words had hurt her. It was killing him to have to sit here making polite dinner conversation with her and her father, when what he really wanted was to take her in his arms and soothe away the pain he'd caused.

He'd been tied in emotional knots by the events of the afternoon. The final straw had been finding her with dinner for two laid out. He'd put all the pieces together and come up with a reconciliation. Even after Melly had described the conditions of their lunching together and stated her feelings about fidelity, he'd still expected to see Marshall come through the door.

She had earned his trust. But could he trust Marshall? Worse yet, could he trust fate not to rekindle the feelings that had drawn Melly to Brian in the first place?

Melissa closed the door behind her father. She was in no hurry to face Morgan. How could he think she was seeing someone else? And how could he have been so cruel as to throw their first kiss in her face as proof that she wasn't trustworthy?

What more could he possibly have to say to her and what on earth was she going to say to him? He was sitting on one end of the couch.

"I have your sweatsuit washed. I've been meaning to give it to you, but I keep forgetting. I'll get it so you can take it home with you."

"I only want to take it home with me if you're in it," he invited.

She stood silently, looking at him. Charm and innuendos weren't going to be enough. This time she needed more.

Morgan stood up and came over to stand in front of her. He reached out, running his hands slowly up and down her arms.

Melissa closed her eyes. The scent of his aftershave flowed over her. The tension in her muscles gradually began to drain away with his soothing touch. She slowly opened her eyes and looked up at him.

"I'm sorry for jumping to conclusions. But after finding out from Marshall that the two of you had had lunch together and then finding you expecting company . . ." His voice was low and filled with a pain that matched her own. "You have every right to be angry at me . . . Hell, I'm angry at myself."

She swallowed, trying to clear the lump out of her throat. "It's not just the anger, Morgan."

"I hurt you, too, didn't I?" He swore. His hands stopped their gentle caresses. "An apology doesn't seem like enough, but it's all I've got." She could see he was hurting, too.

His hands came up to frame her face as he moved

his mouth over hers, his tongue asking for and receiving admittance to the warm recesses of her mouth.

Lifting his head, he looked down at her. "I love you, Melly." His arms slid down around her, pulling her close against him.

"I love you, too, Morgan."

His blue eyes flashed with surprise and wonder. He shook his head in disbelief. "I didn't realize . . ." He smiled down at her.

"Well, I didn't realize you loved me."

"Even after my attack of jealousy this afternoon? The thought of you with Marshall . . ." He didn't finish his sentence, but there was a desperate look in his eyes that told her more than words could have.

"Morgan, Brian is in my past. Whatever there was between us is over, and what I felt for him was never as strong as what I feel for you."

He clutched her tightly to him, burying his head in the curve of her shoulder.

"You have to trust me, Morgan."

"Melly, I do . . . I do trust you. I didn't at first, I'm sorry. But even so, I don't trust Marshall. I think he's up to something and I want you to be careful."

She snuggled against him, feeling his heart beat against her own. He loved her. Her hands splayed over his shoulder blades.

Without warning, Morgan straightened. Lifting her up into his arms, he carried her to the couch and sat down. Cradled on his lap, she smiled up at him, playfully tracing his bottom lip with her finger.

He took hold of her wrist and moved her hand

closer to his mouth so he could kiss her palm. "I'll never forgive myself for what I said about our first kiss . . ." Enfolding her hand in his, he set them both down in her lap.

"*I* forgive you . . ."

"It was one of the most wonderful moments of my life and I made it sound cheap and ugly."

"Was it really one of the most wonderful moments in your life?" She smiled up at him.

"Lady, you knocked the law of gravity right out from under me."

She reached up and kissed him, grateful once again for the knowledge she wasn't the only one so deeply affected by the electricity between them.

Long moments later she pulled back and lay her head down on his shoulder. "I think my father noticed I had been kissed well. He asked if we were getting serious."

Morgan cringed. "I don't know how you kept from pouring my ice water over my head when I said that. What did you tell your father?"

"I told him we'd only been going out several weeks."

"It doesn't sound very long, does it? And I know I gave you a lot of grief over getting engaged to Marshall after only three months . . ."

"But it doesn't *feel* like a couple of weeks. It feels like you've always been a part of me."

"I know," he agreed. "Time frame aside, are we getting serious?"

"*I'm* serious." She lifted herself up and nibbled on his earlobe. "What about you?"

"Very serious." His kiss demonstrated his words.

The last remnants of her hurt and anger dissipated under his tender loving touch. His hands moved over her, soothing—then inflaming.

He shifted until he was able to stretch out full-length on his back. Melissa uncurled herself to lie over him. Then his lips and hands carried her off once more to the timeless realms where forward movement was measured by the increase of her heart-beat and seconds and minutes became meaningless.

"Angel, I've got to go now . . . while I still can."

His voice pulled Melissa from her sensual daze. She opened her eyes and looked down at him.

"Seems to me this isn't the first time I've sat down on a couch with you and ended up in this position."

"It's not." He laughed softly. "At least this time I remember getting here."

She sighed, moving gently against him as she slowly withdrew her hands from underneath his shirt.

Melissa didn't like the thought of reopening old problems, but she couldn't let their relationship move farther along with them unresolved. She didn't want him to doubt that what she was doing was for him and not because of the crush or any of the fantasies she'd had.

"Morgan, remember the other day when you told me you used to pretend you were driving a Ferrari while you were driving your VW?"

"Yes."

"Having a Ferrari was a dream . . . a fantasy."

He retrieved one blond curl that rested on his

shoulder, playfully winding it around his finger. "I suppose."

"Once the Ferrari was within your means you bought it, right?"

"Yes." His eyes narrowed in confusion. "What are you getting at here?"

"Did you ever have trouble distinguishing between your *real* car and the car in your fantasies?"

"Of course not."

She reached out and ran her hand down his cheek. "You are flesh . . ." Continuing down, her fingers pressed against the pulsepoint on his neck. "And blood . . . You're also my yesterday's fantasy and nothing will change that. But I know the difference between my fantasy and you, just like you know the difference between the Ferrari you pretended you had and the car parked outside."

She moved against him and reaching both arms around his neck, pulled him to her for a kiss that showed him just how real she knew he was.

Morgan groaned. "Melly, Carol . . ."

"Carol's not home."

"Yes, she is."

Melissa heard the sound of Carol's key in the front door. Carol was her best friend and she loved her like a sister, but at the moment she wished Carol was on the moon—or anywhere other than getting ready to enter the apartment.

She reluctantly untangled her legs from Morgan's and sat up. Her dress needed a few adjustments to get it back in order.

By the time Carol opened the door, the two of

them were sitting side by side on the couch. The three of them talked briefly before Carol headed for the kitchen and Melissa walked Morgan to the front door.

"Melly, can you get off work early tomorrow?"

"I can probably finish up by three o'clock."

"All right. Let's say I pick you up here at three-thirty and we barbecue at my place?"

"All right."

His good-night kiss was tame compared to those they'd shared earlier, but it was filled with anticipation of things to come.

TWELVE

Today Morgan's living-room drapes were open, revealing sliding-glass doors leading out to a patio. Melissa walked over to the window and looked out. It was a beautiful day—one of those November Indian summer days that transplants to California write home about.

A waist-high wall surrounded the patio, and beyond an expanse of sand stretched out to meet the Pacific Ocean. "I didn't realize you were so close to the beach."

"Right in my front yard."

Morgan slid the door open and stepped out; Melissa followed. A table and chairs sat to one side, a barbecue to the other. Lush plants sprouted out of terra cotta planters scattered along the patio's perimeter.

"Have a seat," Morgan said.

Melissa sat at the table and watched as Morgan lit the barbecue. He was wearing a long-sleeved polo shirt and khaki pants, but her mind kept remembering how he'd looked in his white sweatpants in Palm Springs.

After so many years of living on his own, Morgan was a good cook, but neither of them had much of an appetite. They shared the clean-up chores and then returned to the patio.

Standing next to the wall, they looked out to where the orange sun was sinking into the dark-blue sea.

Melissa sighed.

"Beautiful, isn't it?" Morgan asked. He turned her to face him. "Almost as beautiful as you are."

He closed the space between them. His tongue drew slow, lazy circles around her lips before sweeping into her mouth as his mouth came down hard on hers.

The sun had completely disappeared by the time he broke the kiss. Lifting his head, he looked into her eyes. "I want you, Melissa."

"I want you, too."

"Now?"

"Yes . . . definitely yes." She leaned forward to kiss him again, her mouth opening beneath his. His tongue teased hers as his hands moved down to rub over her nipples that had already grown hard.

Gathering her more tightly into his arms, he buried his face in her hair and groaned. "We'd better go inside before I make love to you out here."

Arms resting around each others' waists, they

moved as one. When they entered his bedroom, Morgan flipped a switch, turning on dim bedside lamps.

The room was beautifully decorated—a study in black and white. Just inside the doorway they stopped and turned to each other, his lips quickly claiming hers. She sighed softly as his kisses moved to her jaw, then up to her temple as he pulled her close, resting his chin on the top of her head.

Melissa buried herself in his chest, planting kisses and nibbling on the warm skin exposed by the open V of his collar. "You taste like charcoal."

He bent and nipped at her earlobe. "So do you. How about a shower?"

"Together?"

"You don't think I'm going to let you out of my reach long enough for us to shower separately, do you?"

"I guess not."

Morgan took her hand and led her into the adjoining bathroom. Once again everything was black and white. The room was large with both a sunken tub and large shower stall.

Morgan adjusted the water in the shower. Satisfied with the temperature, he turned back to Melissa. One by one, he slowly removed each article of her clothing.

He moved back to examine his handiwork. "Too beautiful for words." His hands touched her, following the path of his visual caress.

Melissa put her hands on his hips. Grabbing hold of the bottom of his shirt, she lifted it up over his head. There before her was the glorious chest he'd flaunted her with in Palm Springs. But now it was hers to touch and explore to her heart's delight.

Her fingers moved over him, curling into the dark mat of hair, fluttering over his male nipples, moving down to the waist band of his pants.

Morgan slipped out of his shoes as she tackled his button and zipper. The rest of his clothes joined his shirt. Her eyes slowly moved over him. For a moment she thought she might be dreaming, or drifting through a fantasy. How could a real man be so perfect?

But when he reached out and pulled her to him, there was no doubt in her mind—he was real, he was perfect, and he was hers.

He led her into the shower, pulling her under the running water with him, holding her close. Warm water surrounded them, showering down from three walls.

Melissa's skin tingled where naked flesh met naked flesh. All her nerve endings were sensitized. She could feel each water droplet as it ran over her back and sides.

She looked down at the contrasting ivory softness of her breasts crushed against the tanned hardness of Morgan's chest, his dark hairs curling around to lie across her skin.

A now-familiar shiver rippled through her.

"Water too cold?" Morgan started to reach out to adjust the temperature, but Melissa stopped him.

"Morgan, I never feel cold when I'm near you."

"But you're always shivering."

"I know, but it's not from the cold."

Morgan tipped her chin up and kissed her deeply, moving slowly against her. Her body ached with the need for a fulfillment she'd never had but had imagined many times.

He pulled away from her. She noticed his breathing was as ragged as her own. Picking up the soap, he moved them back out of the direct spray. Then starting at her shoulders, he began to cover her with lather.

He explored thoroughly. When he found an especially sensitive area, he lingered until she quivered beneath his fingers.

He squeezed some shampoo into his palms and then worked it into her hair. His strong but gentle fingers massaged her scalp in small circular movements.

He handed her the shampoo and she repeated the process on his hair. But when she reached for the soap, he stopped her.

"I think I'd better take a rain check on that particular pleasure. Besides, this is faster." He pulled her into his arms, holding her close, the lather creating a slick film between them. When he moved back, he was covered with soap bubbles.

"It worked," Melissa said.

"Of course it worked. Now do my back." He turned his back to her. Holding her hands in his, he pulled her tightly against him.

When he let go of her hands to pull her hips more tightly to him, her hands roamed freely across the muscular stretch of his chest. She placed small kisses across his shoulder blades.

"God, I can't take much more of this," he groaned as he turned back to face her.

His mouth closed over hers, as once again he pulled her under the water. They stayed just long enough to rinse all the soap and shampoo from their bodies.

He led her out of the shower, their discarded clothes the only splash of color amidst the black and white of the bathroom. Morgan gently dried her, then wrapped her in a soft fluffy white towel. He quickly dried himself as well, wrapping the towel around his waist when he finished.

Hand in hand, they walked back into the bedroom. Melissa wasn't sure what to do next. When she was in his arms she felt confident . . . wanted . . . feminine . . . sexy. But now, standing in his bedroom, she was unsure of herself.

She could feel Morgan's eyes on her, but couldn't look at him. She had been so preoccupied with his worrying about living up to her fantasies, she had completely forgotten about her living up to his realities.

How many women had he made love to? What if she disappointed him? He probably assumed, as everyone else seemed to, that she had been sleeping with Brian. She didn't think he was expecting an inexperienced virgin.

Trying to look like she knew what she was doing, Melissa let go of his hand and moved over to the spacious bed to pull back the covers. When she turned, she found Morgan right behind her, close enough that her half step brought her into his arms.

He kissed her gently. "I'll be right back," he whispered against her lips.

"Now what?" she asked the walls, after he'd left the room. She couldn't stand around in his room wearing a towel. She took it off and climbed onto the bed.

It was so quiet, she could hear the sound of the waves crashing on the beach outside. She lay back on the pillow, trying to relax.

She heard footsteps in the hall and her uneasiness intensified. In a flash of modesty, she reached down and pulled the sheet up to the top swells of her breasts.

Morgan entered. "I believe the fantasy called for champagne." He held up an ice bucket with a bottle of champagne. He set it and two glasses next to the bed.

"And candlelight." He took a book of matches out of the nightstand and used them to light candles she hadn't noticed earlier. He turned off the lamps.

"Sorry, no robes, but the sheets are satin . . ." He stood at the side of the bed looking down at her. Droplets of water shimmered in his hair and the dark curls that spread across his chest and below.

The movement of his hands at his waist drew her attention. As he worked the towel loose, her eyes flew up to his face.

"Melly?" he whispered the question. She realized he was giving her one last chance to change her mind. She could stop everything here and now.

But could she? Her love for him was so strong she could no longer contain it within herself, and as the tide rushes in to the shore, her love needed to flow to him.

Her eyes never leaving his, she moved to the center of the bed, folding back the sheet next to her in invitation. Morgan slid in next to her, his towel left on the floor. He moved until the top of his body covered hers. His mouth was inches from her own, his hooded gaze blazing blue fire.

The tension, the anticipation, crackled between them. She had to say something . . . anything to ease the pressure building up within her. "W-w-what about the champagne?"

He moved one hard, muscular thigh across hers. "It's not going anywhere."

Time—she needed time. Her heart was beating so rapidly, it frightened her. They had to slow down . . . she had to slow him down. "I'm not going anywhere, either."

"Yes, you are." He placed a kiss on the side of her neck and whispered in her ear, his voice husky, his breath warm against her skin. "Lady, I'm going to take you to heaven and back."

Like a wave crashing through the walls surrounding a sand castle, his words, his touch, his kisses vanquished all her fears and uncertainties.

By the time he shifted his full weight on top of her, she was so completely aroused that when he first encountered resistance, she didn't remember why.

"God, Melly . . . why didn't you tell me?"

"Morgan, please . . ." She frantically clutched at his back and captured his mouth in a desperate attempt to keep him from stopping.

He returned her kiss. Slipping his hands under her, he slid them lower until they were beneath her hips. Lifting her up to meet his downward thrust, he made her his.

He moved slowly at first, making sure she was feeling only pleasure before he opened the floodgates of his own passion. Filling her with new sensations, he fed the hunger he'd created in her from the first time he'd kissed her.

The sound of the sea grew louder, pounding in her ears until she became one with it, crashing again and again, drowning in sensual delight. From far off she heard a cry of triumph . . . answered by another voice calling out her name.

Melissa was still drifting in the uprush of their passion when Morgan blew out the candles.

In the darkness, he gathered her to him, cradling her head on his shoulder.

"I wish you had told me."

"What difference would it have made?"

"I'm not sure." His hands ran slowly up and down her back. "But there must have been something I could have done to make it more memorable . . . more special. The first time should be special." He kissed the top of her head.

"It was special." She turned in his arms, until she could lean forward and kiss him. "Nothing could have made it better."

He surrendered to her kiss, but only for a short time. "Angel, you need to get some sleep."

"But I'm not tired."

Morgan laughed and took hold of her wrist to keep her hand from moving any further down his abdomen. "Believe me, you should have at least a few hours' rest."

"Because it was the first time?"

"Yes."

She settled back down against him. "Are you disappointed?"

"God, no. I can't describe quite how I feel. Ecstatic, deeply honored, grateful . . . maybe. But disappointed . . . not at all."

Melissa sighed contentedly, and drifted off to sleep.

The first thing she heard in the morning was the roar of the ocean and the distant cry of a gull. She thought she was sleeping with her back against the wall, but then remembered her bed wasn't near a wall.

Her eyes flew open. She saw the black-and-white decor and remembered . . . everything.

The wall must be Morgan.

What did a woman say to a man after they'd spent the night together? It had been so easy in the intimacy of candlelight and in the darkness of early morning when they'd both awakened and made love again, but now it was daylight and this was all so new to her. . . .

Morgan stirred. His arms came around her and hugged her body to his before he rolled her over onto her back.

"Good morning." He leaned over and kissed her.

Pulling back, he looked down at her. "How are you feeling?"

"Still a bit overwhelmed." Her heartbeat raced as she saw the spark of desire flame in his eyes.

"Me, too, angel . . . me, too." He placed soft kisses on her forehead, nose, and chin.

"I love you, Morgan."

"Me, too." He ran the tip of his finger along the line of her slightly swollen bottom lip.

"I'm still trying to get used to the idea." She nipped at his finger.

"I'll give you all the time you need to get used to it, and all the proof you can handle."

This time, in the flushed afterglow of lovemaking, instead of the desire to curl up and sleep, Melissa found she felt like getting up and conquering the world. She settled for helping Morgan fix breakfast.

Dressed in one of his shirts that hit her midthigh, she sat across the kitchen table from him.

Morgan set his now-empty coffee cup on the table. "I wish every day could start off the way today has. Waking up with you in my arms, making love to you, having breakfast . . ." He reached across the table and took her hand. "Melly, move in with me."

Melissa liked the idea of being able to repeat this morning again, too—and, of course, last night. Carol had been expecting her to move out in January anyway and had already made plans to turn her bedroom into an exercise room, so she didn't have to worry about that.

In Palm Springs, Morgan had said he might never

settle down. To her, living together was settling down. Was it for him? "It's a pretty big commitment . . . Are you sure?"

"I'm sure it's what I want, but if you think it's too much too fast, we can hold off. I'll understand."

"Nothing about this relationship has moved at normal speed. Why should we start now?" She smiled at him and squeezed his hand.

Melissa ended up moving only her clothes and personal items. Although some of the furniture in the apartment was hers, she left it with Carol for the time being.

She and Morgan spent their time at home together much as they had the first day—being together, discovering each other. They touched often—a short friendly hug here, a long, more than friendly hug there. The passion between them surfaced frequently.

As the love between them grew deeper, so did their friendship. More and more Melissa found herself looking forward to the end of each workday, and, of course, the weekend.

A week after she'd moved in, Morgan sat behind the desk at his office staring off into blank space. He was in love with Melly. She was in love with him.

He hadn't realized how empty and lonely the apartment had been until she'd moved in.

Just knowing that he was in love filled him with wonder—he'd been so sure he would never love again after Emmie, but here he was.

Once he'd realized he was in love, everything had

fallen into place: the pain he'd felt when he was trying to stay away from her, his willingness to put his pride on the line, the way she haunted his thoughts, his total lack of interest in other women, his intense reaction when he'd thought she was having Marshall over for dinner, the physical reaction her slightest touch evoked in him, his obsession with being her best lover.

And he was her only lover. To say he'd been surprised would be a major understatement. He still couldn't describe how he felt about it, but it was one of the most fulfilling emotions he'd ever experienced. It was a gift to him . . . a gift a woman can give only once, and Melly had given it to him.

"Mr. Edwards, Ms. Ellison is on line one." His secretary's voice, over the intercom broke into his thoughts.

He picked up the phone. "Melly, I was just thinking about you."

"Good thoughts, I hope."

"Always."

"I've been thinking about you, too. The roses are beautiful! Thank you."

"Roses?" *Roses?* Someone had sent Melly roses? He knew he hadn't done it. "Was there a card?"

"Yes, it said 'Happy Anniversary' just as you'd instructed. It's really sweet of you to remember that it's been a week since I moved in with you."

"Actually I was thinking about how wonderful this past week has been when you called." Anniversary roses? Could be a mixup at the florists, but he had a hunch they were from Marshall. "But I'm afraid I can't take credit for the roses."

Silence followed his remark.

"Melly?"

"You didn't send the roses." She sounded disappointed. "I wonder who did?"

"Someone close enough for you to count anniversaries with."

"Let me get my appointment book." He heard the sound of papers shuffling. "The ninth, today's the ninth . . ." He could hear more shuffling, then a quick intake of breath. "Listen, I'm sorry I bothered you at work. I'll see you at home."

"Melly, who are the flowers from?"

"I don't know for sure, but I think they might be from Brian. We met on the ninth of July."

"Can't say that I'm surprised."

"Well, I am! I haven't seen him or talked to him since we had lunch last week."

"Listen, since it is our one-week anniversary, why don't I pick you up in an hour and we'll go out to lunch to celebrate?" Plus he'd stop by the jeweler's on his way and pick up some earrings or a necklace to commemorate the occasion. Maybe he'd take a look at engagement rings while he was there.

"Okay," she said, then added softly, "I'm sorry about the roses."

"No need for you to apologize. You didn't send them."

He hung up the phone. Gray clouds had appeared on his euphoric horizon. Once again he was reminded that there were never any guarantees with love. It was like being in the Coliseum waiting for a thumbs-up or thumbs-down from Caesar.

He realized just how much he had at risk, how much he had on the line. It wasn't just his pride anymore . . . it was his life.

THIRTEEN

"Roses, for me?" Carol exclaimed.

"I can't take them home or keep them in my office, but I couldn't bring myself to throw them away." Melissa entered the apartment and handed the roses to Carol.

Carol looked confused. "Why can't you keep them? Have you developed an allergy to roses?"

"They're from Brian."

"I see." Carol walked over and set the flowers on the dining-room table.

"They came with a card that said 'Happy Anniversary.' "

Carol whistled. "Guess you haven't told him about Morgan."

"It isn't any of his business. I'm not prying into his love life." She hadn't told anyone other than Carol and her immediate family about Morgan. Her relationship with Brian had been such a public media circus, and she knew if too many people knew about her and Morgan, there was a chance the press might pick up on it, too.

"According to the papers Brian hasn't had much of a love life lately, other than taking you to lunch last week."

"Morgan thinks Brian wants me back." They'd discussed it briefly over lunch. Morgan insisted she was being naive if she thought all Brian wanted from her was friendship.

Carol looked pointedly at the roses. "He might be right."

"Not you, too?"

"Lissa, why else would he have sent anniversary flowers?"

"I don't know, but I plan to ask him. I tried calling him earlier, but he wasn't in. I talked to his mother."

"Yuck."

Melissa laughed. "Well, she's not my favorite person, either, but she's much easier to put up with now that we're not about to be related. So, are you ready to go Christmas shopping?"

After several hours of shopping, they went back to the apartment. Melissa offered to help Carol carry her packages in. As they headed up the walkway they saw a man move away from the apartment door and start toward them.

"Expecting company?" Melissa asked Carol.

"No."

When the man stepped into a patch of light spilling out of an apartment window, Melissa recognized Brian.

"Hi. Here let me take those." Before either woman could protest, Brian gathered up all the packages. "Getting ready for the holidays?"

Carol opened the apartment door and the three of them entered. At Carol's direction, Brian put the packages on the dining-room table, next to the roses.

"Anyone for coffee?" Carol asked.

Melissa looked at her watch. Morgan had had a meeting with a client at eight o'clock, but expected to be home by nine-thirty. She had wanted to be home when he got there, but technically speaking Brian was her company even though this was no longer her home, so how could she leave?

"Coffee sounds fine, Carol."

"I see you got the roses," Brian said, once they were alone.

"Yes, thank you, Brian, they're beautiful."

"Glad you like them, but I'm afraid I didn't send them."

Brian hadn't sent the roses? "But you just said, 'I see you got the roses?' "

"In a way I guess they are from me, since I paid for them, but Mother is the one who ordered them."

"I see."

"Old habits die hard, Lissa. She's still trying to run my life. When she gave me the message that you'd called, she confessed what she'd done. She wants us married before she goes back to Chicago. She even went so far as to make up this crazy story about running into you leaving a restaurant with Morgan Edwards.'' He laughed.

Why did he think the news had been fabricated? ''She didn't make it up, it happened.''

Brian looked stunned. ''But that was just a few weeks after I'd called off the engagement.''

Ah—he didn't like the idea of her dating so soon after their breakup. She wondered what he would think about her living with Morgan? Not that she was going to tell him. As she'd told Carol, her life wasn't any of his business. ''So? Is there some kind of official mourning period following broken engagements that I'm not aware of?''

''No, of course not. I just assumed . . .'' He shrugged his shoulders. ''Listen, would you like to take in a movie Saturday night?''

''Why?'' His invitation had been so unexpected, the question popped out before she had time to think.

''Because I enjoy your company and like spending time with you. I thought we were still friends.''

''We are, but I don't think our going out together is a good idea.''

''Because of my mother's interfering.''

''No, I just don't see us as being friends in the sense that we would go places together. Face it, Brian, if we went out to the movies Saturday night, it would be all over the papers Sunday and the hot topic on David Andrews' show on Monday.'' Not to mention she had her own plans to spend Saturday evening with Morgan . . . and they didn't involve going to the movies.

*   *   *

The next evening Morgan came in as she was starting dinner. "Hi, how was your day?"

"Business or personal?"

"Well, business, of course. Your personal day is just beginning." She winked at him.

Fighting back a smile, he shook his head. "Not quite true today." He set his briefcase on the table, opened it, and pulled out a newspaper.

He handed it to Melissa. Circled in red was a gossip-column blurb about Brian sending her roses for the anniversary of their meeting, and a general rehashing of their entire relationship.

"I'll bet Beverly called the newspaper after she called the florist."

"I wouldn't doubt it." He leaned back against the kitchen counter. "We could foil her little campaign by developing our own high social profile."

"But I don't like this kind of thing." With a look of disgust, she dropped the newspaper back into his briefcase.

"Well then, maybe we should get married. That would stop the speculations of your reconciling with Brian."

Thoughts of marrying Morgan had been flitting through her mind on a regular basis, but she had been dismissing them as flashbacks from old fantasies. She realized now, that, yes, she would be willing to make a lifetime commitment to this man—a commitment based on love and her desire to share the rest of her life with him, *not* as a convenient way to keep her name from being linked with Brian's in the newspapers.

Disappointment fought with anger at his casual attitude to such a major step in their relationship. Anger won. "That's the worst reason for getting married I've ever heard!"

Morgan raised his eyebrows. "Fine. Suit yourself." He straightened, walked to the table, picked up the newspaper, and tossed it across the room into the trash. Then before picking up his briefcase, he slammed the lid of it closed. "Don't bother fixing anything for me. I've lost my appetite."

"Me, too." She started to storm past him, but he reached out and pulled her to him. She glared up at him.

He set his briefcase back down and wrapped his arms around her, his hands running gently over her back, kneading away the knots of tension.

"Melly, if we both end up sulking this evening, then Beverly is winning."

Melissa took a deep breath. He was right. She returned his hug, holding him close to her, feeling his heartbeat next to her own. The first flutters of desire quivered through her. Pulling back slightly, she looked up at him. "What if I sulk this evening and you can have tomorrow evening?" she teased.

"Then she's won twice. Why don't we agree that nobody gets to sulk?"

"Guess I'd better get dinner going then." She started to take a step back, but he pulled her in closer to him.

"Not necessarily." His kiss was powerful and possessive, wiping out all thoughts of Brian, Beverly, the press, dinner, and anything else beyond the two of them and the primal bond that tied them to each other.

Her plans for starting her own business were moving along. She was looking at office space and putting out feelers for prospective clients.

Morgan was expanding his business, adding staff and forming a permanent home office. While he would still be traveling, his nomadic days were over. He was giving up some of the freedom of working alone free-lance so he could take on a greater number of projects, as well as more complex projects.

Since they were both so busy, their time together was limited, but cherished.

The holidays came and went in a flurry of family gatherings. Mitch made comments and dropped hints about grandchildren, but otherwise little was said about their relationship.

Brian stopped by the store every now and then, and somehow the press always seemed to pick up on it. Melissa wasn't sure if Beverly was the instigator, or if it was Brian himself. He called and stopped by the apartment, too, but Carol told him she was out. He didn't seem to suspect that she no longer lived there.

She didn't know if Morgan was seeing the newspaper items or not. He was staying silent on the subject and she didn't want to bring it up. She was reluctant to waste any of their precious time together with unpleasantness.

The Friday before what would have been their wedding day, Brian made another of his visits to her.

They talked for half an hour in her office. After she refused his offer of lunch, he left and she got back to the business at hand—trying to decide what to do with one hundred and twenty hot-pink basketballs.

She'd barely had time to pull out a legal pad and sharpen a pencil before her door opened and another visitor entered.

"Guess we'll be reading about you in the papers . . . again." Morgan closed the door and came across the room to stand in front of her desk. "How long is this going to go on, Melly?"

"How long is what going to go on?" She was pretty sure he must have seen Brian leaving, but she wanted to be sure before she answered him.

"Marshall's little visits." His arms were crossed tightly across his chest.

"Brian's my friend. He's got a lot going on in his life right now, dealing with his celebrity status and trying to handle his mother. He needs someone to talk to."

"There are plenty of competent paid professionals to help him with his problems. It's not your job!"

"I don't consider friendship a job." She stood up and while she still couldn't face him eye-to-eye, she didn't have to look up quite so far.

"Then let him find some other friends. I don't like you spending so much time with your *ex*-fiancé." He uncrossed his arms, placed his hands on her desk and leaned toward her. "Have you even told him about us yet?"

She had wanted eye-to-eye, but now that she had it she wasn't sure she wanted it. She shifted her weight from one foot to the other. "No. I don't discuss my private life with him."

"But he's such a *good* friend . . ." His voice was calm, but his eyes flashed his anger.

"Not that good a friend."

"Maybe you don't want him to know that you're serious about someone else. Maybe you want him to think you're still available. Maybe in your mind you are still available." His hands clenched into fists, his knuckles showing white.

"How can you say that? We're living together."

"With what little you moved in, you could be packed and out of there in an afternoon!"

A shadow of fear swept over her, then settled around her heart. "Are you saying that you want me to move out?"

Looking shocked, he straightened up to his full height. "No. What I want is a guarantee that I won't come home from work some evening to find you and your belongings gone. I think it's time we . . ."

He was going to do it again. She could feel it coming. He was going to propose again, this time out of anger *and* jealousy. "Don't you dare ask me to marry you as some kind of a guarantee!"

The cynical look on his face showed that marriage was the last thing he had in mind. "I wasn't going to."

Melissa looked down at her desk, wishing she could crawl under it. *Oh, well, it could have been worse—he could have laughed*.

"I was going to say that it was time we made sure Brian knew about the two of us and that since you don't seem to want to tell him, then perhaps we should show him.''

She looked up quickly. ''How?''

''Marshall House will be finished soon and he's planning an open house. I want you to go with me.''

Brian had mentioned the open house to her. She had assumed Morgan wouldn't want her going, and was surprised that he did. ''Planning to flaunt me like the prize out of a cereal box?''

''No, I want you by my side showing support for my accomplishments.''

''Morgan, I know most of Brian's friends—don't you think it might be a bit awkward.''

''Only if you still have feelings for him.'' He was watching her intently.

She sighed. ''We've been through this before.''

''Yes, I know.'' He closed his eyes, running both hands through his hair. When he looked back at her, she could easily read the frustration on his face. ''But you say one thing, Melly, while your actions suggest just the opposite.''

Melissa caught her bottom lip between her teeth. She hated to admit it, but looking at things from Morgan's perspective, she could see how he might reach the conclusion that there really was still something between her and Brian.

''Fine, if my going to the open house with you will solve this issue once and for all, I'll do it.''

He was driving her crazy! Morgan had been tense and irritable all week. Melissa wondered if this was

an artist's moodiness before the unveiling of his finished product or if it was related to her and Brian.

He seemed possessed with nervous energy. He rarely
just sat and relaxed anymore. At home, he was either
up doing something or working in his study.

At breakfast the Monday morning before the
event, she asked what he would be wearing to the
open house.

His muscles tensed visibly. "Why?"

"Well . . . I'm going shopping for a dress on my
lunch hour and I thought I'd get something to
match."

"Hell, I don't know what I'm wearing!" he
exploded.

She was shocked that he'd raised his voice to
her—he'd never done that before. "I also thought
since I'd be at the mall," she continued cautiously,
"I'd pick up the housewarming gift. Brian and I saw
a pewter figure of a baseball player one day and I
thought—"

Morgan scowled. "You thought you could give it
to him and he can think of you every time he sees
it."

"No . . . no, I hadn't meant that at all. I was only
trying to think of something I knew he would like."

His eyes were cold. "I always give my clients a
framed copy of my original concept drawing of their
building. Marshall will get the same. I'll include
your name on the card," he said stiffly.

Something was definitely bothering him. Hopefully, if it was her friendship with Brian, everything
would be resolved at the open house. If it wasn't,
she didn't know what she'd do.

_____ FOURTEEN _____

Saturday, Morgan had been even more edgy than he had during the past week. He was quiet, almost sulky, as they got ready for the open house.

He usually made a wickedly suggestive comment about her outfit before they went out for an evening, but tonight he ignored her new silver dress.

Morgan looked heartstoppingly gorgeous in his formal evening wear. Standing in front of him, Melissa ran her hands over the smooth fabric covering his shoulders.

"Maybe we should stay home. I don't know if I want other women anywhere near you. You could easily become the first architect to have groupies," she teased.

He frowned. "Melissa, this evening is business for me, not a social event. Are you ready to go?"

Her smile faded. "Yes. I'm ready."

*   *   *

Quite a few people were already there when they arrived. The parking attendant took Morgan's car and the two of them stood looking at Marshall House.

The exterior of the house was well lit, with an artist's eye for shadow and composition. "It's beautiful, Morgan."

"Glad you like it," he acknowledged her compliment stiffly. "Shall we go in?"

They were standing only inches from each other, but he seemed miles away. Melissa moved closer to his side, tucking her arm around his. "I'm proud of you." She smiled up at him.

She could feel the tension draining away from him, see the tightness in his face relax and the shadows fade from his eyes. "Thank you, angel." He smiled back at her, kissed her gently on the lips, then turned her to him and kissed the side of her neck.

"I love you," she whispered next to his ear.

His arms slid around her back, pulling her so tightly against him that it took her a moment to catch her breath. "I love you, too," he returned.

When she heard the parking attendant returning, Melissa moved back to Morgan's side and they walked up the steps to the front door.

The door was opened by a uniformed maid who let them into the spacious entry hall. Brian was there greeting guests. Just behind him stood an easel, holding Morgan's drawing.

When Brian looked up and saw the two of them,

a flicker of surprise passed over his features, before he headed in their direction.

"And here's the man of the hour now, folks . . . Edwards . . ." He reached out and shook Morgan's hand. "I hope you brought plenty of business cards with you. Everyone loves the house."

He turned to Melissa. "You're looking gorgeous as always, Lissa." He smiled, his eyes moving appreciatively over her.

"Thank you. The house is beautiful, Brian."

"Have Edwards show you the rest of it. Although it's hard to see much, with so many people here."

As the maid let more guests in the front door, Brian moved on to greet them. She and Morgan went into the living room.

She knew many of the people there. Everyone was friendly toward her, but she knew there was a lot of speculation about her presence. It was hard not to notice the whispered conversations going on with furtive glances in her direction.

Beverly spoke with them briefly, then flitted off to mingle elsewhere.

Melissa stayed close to Morgan. Although they weren't always talking to the same group of people, she was always within several arm lengths of him.

Morgan was talking to the owner of the Conquistadors when Brian came up behind her.

Leaning close to her he asked, "So what do you think of the house?"

"What I've seen of it is beautiful."

"Hasn't Edwards shown you around?"

"We're slowly making progress."

"Come on. I'll take you on a personal tour."

Melissa looked over at Morgan. He was still deeply involved in his conversation, but several of the other people in the area had heard Brian's offer and were watching her.

Either way—whether she accepted or refused—there was bound to be talk. Since she did want to see the rest of the house, she accepted.

With one hand supporting her elbow, he led her through the crowd. Plenty of speculative looks followed them as they went from room to room. When he turned down an empty hallway, Melissa stopped. She knew the master bedroom suite lay beyond the single door at the end.

"Looks like this end of the house is off limits."

"It is for everyone else."

"Then maybe we should turn back."

"Aren't you curious to see how it came out? After all, this was almost your house, too." With his hand at the small of her back, he urged her forward.

When they reached the door, he opened it and stood back for her to enter.

Melissa walked into the master bedroom. Brian closed the door behind them.

"Well, what do you think?" Brian asked.

"It's beautiful, just like the rest of the house. The interior designer did a wonderful job."

"You picked her out," he reminded her softly.

She walked over to the fireplace. Standing in front of it, she ran her hand across the cool marble of the mantel.

This had almost been her bedroom. The man

behind her had almost been her husband. On the surface it might look like she'd given up a lot, but compared to the love she had with Morgan, it was nothing.

"I'm glad you decided to come after all."

"Brian, I came with Morgan."

"Well, he is a family friend."

He didn't seem to understand that she and Morgan were not here just as friends. As she walked away from the fireplace, her heels clicking loudly on the tile hearth prevented either of them from hearing the sound of the door opening.

"Brian . . ." she began tentatively.

"Lissa, the past few months have been hell for me." He came to stand in front of her. "I made a mistake when I called off our wedding. It's so clear to me now, especially seeing you here in our bedroom."

Melissa was stunned. Morgan had been right. It seemed Brian did want more than friendship from her. "Brian, I don't know what to say."

Resting one hand on her waist, he used the other to tip her chin up. "I'd like you to say that you still love me and still want to be my wife." He looked down at her hopefully, then began to lower his head to kiss her.

Melissa turned her head to discourage the kiss. When she did, she saw Morgan standing in the doorway.

Her gasp got Brian's attention and his head turned in the direction she was looking.

For long tension-filled moments, Morgan stood

silently looking at them. She had never seen him look so angry.

She started toward him, but he closed the door between them.

She turned back to Brian. "Brian, I appreciate your offer, but . . ." She tried to think of a way to soften her refusal.

"No need to say anything, honey. A picture is worth a thousand words and the looks on your faces said it all."

"I . . . I've got to go." She hated to leave him so abruptly, but she had to get to Morgan. Giving him a small smile, she left the room.

She looked everywhere for Morgan. Spotting him in a crowd should be easy with his height and his jet-black hair, but she had no success. Could he have left?

She fought her way through the thick crowd as best she could—politely but firmly, excusing herself away from people who tried to stop her to talk.

She arrived on the front porch just in time to see Morgan's car disappearing down the drive. She swore softly under her breath.

The door opened behind her and Brian stepped out. "He left?"

"He left."

"Would it help if I said I was sorry?"

"It's not your fault, Brian."

"I knew the two of you had been dating, but I didn't realize there was anything serious between you."

"It's okay." She patted his arm. He hadn't intentionally caused trouble for her.

"Is there anything I can do to help? Maybe if I talked to him?"

"That won't be necessary." Brian looked relieved and she couldn't blame him. Morgan had looked positively thunderous as he'd stormed off. "But I would appreciate it if you could call me a taxi."

"I've got a better idea. My agent rented a limo for the evening. He won't be leaving for a while. Why don't you borrow it?"

"No, really a taxi will be fine."

"I insist. It's the least I can do. I'm sure Jim won't mind."

"You're sure?"

"Yes. It's much more comfortable than a taxi." He took her arm and walked her down the front steps to where the parking attendants were waiting.

When the limousine arrived, Brian helped her in. "I do hope everything works out for you, but if it doesn't, my offer still stands," he told her before closing the door and giving the driver the high sign.

Melissa gave the driver the address, then settled back for the ride.

She wasn't sure Morgan had gone back to the apartment, but her car was there so it made sense to look there first. That way, if she had to look elsewhere, she would have her own transportation.

Even more than she wanted to find Morgan waiting for her at home, she hoped that wherever he'd gone, he'd arrived safely. There was so much power in his car and he'd been so upset.

When she arrived home, her heart sank. She found nothing but darkness waiting for her.

Where would he have gone? To the office? Or maybe he was in the bedroom sleeping? Sleeping? . . . She didn't think so. She started into the living room, heading for the bedroom to see if he was there.

He heard footsteps outside the door, then the sounds of someone entering. Melly. He could smell the light scent of her perfume all the way across the dark room.

He reached over and turned on the end-table lamp next to him. She was alone. That surprised him.

"Well, I knew you'd be back for your things, but I didn't expect you quite so soon." Morgan's voice was so cold and hard he almost didn't recognize it himself.

Rage and pain warred within him. When she'd stood in front of Marshall House and told him she was proud of him and that she loved him, he'd been on top of the world. And he'd stayed there until, out of the corner of his eye, he'd seen her go off with Marshall.

It had taken him a while to wind up the conversation he was having and follow them. It had been a hunch to check the master bedroom. He wished he'd been wrong . . . God, he wished he'd been wrong. But when he'd opened the door they'd been there. Jealousy, pain, and despair had all shot through him, along with the urge to break Brian's neck. An urge he might have given in to if he hadn't left when he had.

Melly walked slowly toward him. "Morgan, I . . ."

He didn't want to hear what she had to say. Didn't want to hear her thank him like Emmie had. Didn't want to hear how sorry she was.

Her eyes fixed on the crystal whiskey decanter sitting on the coffee table in front of him. "You've been drinking?"

"No. I thought about it. But you're not worth the hangover." He stood up.

Her eyes showed the pain his words had caused her. Minor pain compared to what she had done to him. Part of him was glad he had hurt her, and part of him ached to take her into his arms and kiss the hurt away.

But she didn't want his arms or his kisses anymore. She wanted Marshall.

"So, the glory boy's ready to settle down."

"He thinks so." Her answer was soft, quiet.

"Looks like you've won the game then. You gave him time and space and he came back to you."

"Morgan—" She started to speak, but he cut her off.

"How convenient that I was close by to help you pass the time. And I'll bet my having been your first crush really put the icing on your cake. It gave you the chance to live out your girlhood fantasies."

"I thought we'd settled that argument." She moved closer.

Morgan ignored her statement. "You must be real proud. Sweet innocent young girl grows up into beautiful scheming woman and conquers the object of her first crush. Film at eleven, folks.''

The blood drained from her face—another point for him.

''Your sarcasm isn't necessary, Morgan.''

''What in the hell did you expect? That I would graciously help you pack your bags and send you off with a smile and wishes for a happy future? Only in your fantasies, angel . . . only in your fantasies. It's time to put your fantasies to rest now. Welcome to the real world.''

As he looked down at her, desire shot through him. How could he still want her so badly, knowing she was going to leave him?

He came around the coffee table to stand in front of her. ''I hope Marshall's not expecting you back tonight.'' One arm circled her waist and pulled her firmly against him. With his other hand he reached behind her and cradled her head in his hand, as she leaned back to look up at him with troubled eyes. ''Because tonight you're still mine. One last night, angel. One more night . . .''

He moved his mouth down to hers. Small, teasing kisses and nips at her bottom lip until she relaxed in his arms. Once he felt her surrender, he deepened the kiss. The now-familiar taste of her inflamed his desire.

He swept her up into his arms.

''Morgan—'' she started the moment his lips left hers.

He kissed her again. He didn't want to give her

the chance to talk him out of making love to her. He needed this last night together.

He carried her into the bedroom, turning on the lights as he walked through the door. Standing next to the bed he set her down in front of him.

Reaching behind her he found the zipper of her dress. "You have excellent taste. The men couldn't keep their eyes off you in this dress." He lowered the zipper, then moved the dress slowly downward until it lay in a silver pool at her feet.

One eyebrow rose in question as his eyes blazed over her. "Well . . . it's not just the dress that was new." He ran his fingers over the lace that trimmed the iridescent gray teddy she had on. Had she put it on for him or Marshall? No matter, he was the one who was taking it off.

Several times as he was doing just that, she'd tried to talk to him. Each time he'd silenced her with kisses.

Once he had her undressed, he laid her gently on the bed. He sent his clothes to join hers on the floor and he joined her on the bed. She watched him warily, her bottom lip caught between her teeth.

"I was your first crush . . . and the first man to make love to you. That should be enough to ensure that you never forget me, but just in case it's not . . . I guarantee you'll never forget tonight."

She was so sweetly responsive to his every touch. As he sought to spark her passion with his hands and mouth, she was doing the same to him. She might be leaving him, but she obviously wanted this last night as much as he did.

When his experience of her body told him the time was right, he moved one of her legs on either side of him, and knelt before her. His hands moved slowly along the length of her outer thighs. His gaze burned over her as he silently committed her vision to memory.

"Morgan."

He looked up to her face. Her face was framed by the soft curling disarray of her hair, her eyes looked haunted. But still they burned with desire—desire for him, not Marshall. And her sweet mouth, swollen from his kisses, had just whispered his name.

"Why, Melly? Why?" The question was torn from him.

He watched her eyes fill with tears. He envied her that outlet.

"Melly, how can you walk away from what we have together?"

"I can't." She had spoken softly, but he was sure he'd heard her correctly.

"You can't?" He looked disbelieving.

"I can't leave you, Morgan."

"You're not leaving?" It wasn't quite sinking in.

She moved her hands to cover his hands where they lay still against her. "I'm not leaving."

"What made you change your mind?"

"I didn't change my mind. I never intended to leave."

He could hardly believe it. She wasn't leaving. "Why didn't you tell me?"

She sat up, putting her arms around his neck. Her hot tears flowed freely now, running down his chest.

"I would have told you right away, but you haven't let me get a word in edgewise."

His hands and arms were shaking as he clutched her tightly to him. Burying his head in her hair, he gasped for breath.

"Morgan, it's you I want—who I've always wanted." Her lips were warm against his neck as she kissed him.

When the flow of tears slowed, he pulled back and wiped the last remnants of them from her eyes.

"How could you think I wanted anyone else?" The uneven catch in her voice tore at his heart.

"I heard Brian propose to you."

"I wouldn't have accepted. You should have known that."

She was right, he should have known. He'd trusted her, but each time he found out that she'd seen Marshall it had been harder and harder for him. He realized that once again Emmie had been between them like a watermark on glass—blurring his vision, even when he didn't focus on it.

It was time to remove the last barriers between them—to shatter the glass.

He lay back on the bed, pulling her down on top of him. He told her about Emmie and Robert.

She listened quietly as it all poured out of him—the joy destroyed by betrayal, the pain, the heartache, the vows to never let it happen again.

"Morgan, I'm not Emmie and Brian's not Robert," she said quietly.

His hands played over the smooth skin of her back. "Part of me knew that, but another part of me just couldn't seem to let go of the idea that you were going back to Marshall.''

She lifted her head and looked down into his eyes. He saw her love for him there, as he had many times before. But this time he saw more clearly. No walls—not even glass walls—separated them.

She ran one soft finger along his jaw. ''Does all of you know now that I'm yours?''

He nodded. Yes, he knew she was his. She would always be his . . . just like he would always be hers.

Many times he had given her his body and his heart, but tonight, as he made love to her, he gave her his soul.

Melissa woke the next morning to find Morgan watching her.

''About time you woke up, sleepyhead.'' He smiled down at her.

''I didn't get much sleep.'' Despite the emotionally draining evening, they had spent many hours making love. Knowing about Morgan's ex-fiancée cleared up so many of the questions she'd had about his puzzling behavior. The ghosts were all laid to rest now.

''I didn't get much sleep, either.'' He leaned over and kissed her.

''Then why are you awake?'' She yawned.

He reached behind him to the nightstand and grabbed a manila folder. He opened it, took out a stack of papers, and spread them across the bed in front of her.

They were drawings of houses.

"Take your pick," he said.

"What are they for?" She picked up a sketch of a Victorian-style house, admiring the exquisite detailing.

"For us." Morgan's hand moved in front of the drawing. Between his thumb and forefinger was a diamond ring.

Melissa turned quickly to look at him.

"Marry me, angel?"

"To stop the rumors?"

"No, because I love you."

She threw her arms around his neck and kissed him, thoroughly.

"I take it that's a yes?"

She nodded. He moved back and slipped the ring onto her finger. "When?" she asked him.

"Valentine's Day is a few weeks away. Think we can arrange a small family wedding by then? Unless you want a big fancy wedding with all the trimmings, but that will take more time."

The day already had special meaning for them. "Valentine's Day is perfect. What do you think about having hot fudge sundaes with the wedding cake?"

He laughed. "Whatever you want. We'll get started on the plans first thing Monday morning."

"I could start today."

"You're all booked up for today."

"I am?"

He nodded seriously, but she saw the playful gleam in his eyes. "Rehearsals, angel . . ."

"Rehearsals?"

He rolled over, moving her beneath him. "Rehearsals for the honeymoon."